Neon Hemlock Press
www.neonhemlock.com
@neonhemlock

© Stories copyrighted 2020-2021
© 2022 for anthology as a whole

Baffling Year One
edited by dave ring, Craig L. Gidney & Gabriella Etoniru

Cover Illustration by Molk Tae
Cover Design and Layout by dave ring
Interior Illustrations by Robin Ha

Print ISBN-13: 978-1-952086-52-6
Ebook ISBN-13: 978-1-952086-53-3

edited by dave ring, Craig L. Gidney & Gabriella Etoniru
BAFFLING YEAR ONE

Neon Hemlock Press

Baffling
Year One

EDITED BY DAVE RING
CRAIG L. GIDNEY & GABRIELLA ETONIRU

CONTENTS

Editor's Notes

ISSUE ONE

ISSUE TWO

ISSUE THREE

ISSUE FOUR

Contributors
About the Magazine / About the Press

EDITOR'S NOTES

IN THE FIRST issue of *Baffling*, I wrote: "The Queer Weird aesthetic exists in the fiction of Samuel R Delany and the late Randal Kenan, the works of Jeanette Winterson and the British playwright Joe Orton... The work in Baffling Magazine is very much in the same vein with these master practitioners of interstitial fiction."

Now, a year later, I think we've amassed a group of stories and writers that not only fit that aesthetic, they refine it. You'll find stories that bite, stories that sparkle. Stories that disturb, and stories that make you laugh. The palette ranges from straight up horror (Nino Cipri's "Velvet"', to hopepunk (Jewelle Gomez's "Merida, Yucatan"); from humorous vignettes (Rem Wigmore's "Why We Make Monsters") to work that's experimental and challenges the narrative form (A.B. Young's "Peat Moss and Oil for Burning").

Baffling Magazine is a mad laboratory of queer speculative fiction. It is also very much a labor of love. Both from the authors, who place their words with jewel-like precision to the editors who carefully collect the stories, to the artists who create such beautiful covers. I'd like to think we are community, bolstered by the Patreon supporters of this tiny operation.

Year One is an archive of where we've been. Please join us as we fill the archive for *Year Two*! There's an explosion of queer speculative fiction coming out from both the small and major presses. I'd like to think that *Baffling* is on the vanguard.

Craig L. Gidney, Co-Editor
November 2021

R EADERS, I FELL in love with the short story my sophomore year of college and flash fiction shortly thereafter, amazed by writers' ability to be so poignant and provocative within such small spaces. I greatly appreciate the way in which flash fiction is able to unravel slowly and intensely all at once, the ways in which I'm thrown headfirst into brand new worlds and brought out moments later. I spend much longer mulling over a genius short story than I do reading it, and I firmly believe this power of the short story is what keeps me coming back.

As a nonfiction writer, I don't often get to explore the speculative or fantastical even though the genre is perhaps my favorite to read. And as a Queer writer, I am so often operating as an *other* voice in the spaces I function. I am the Black Queer voice rather than one of many. Working with *Baffling* this past year has been such an immense pleasure. I cannot overstate how fortunate I am to work alongside such talented editors—dave and Craig—and be privy to the riveting, heartfelt, and wonderfully queer writing from our authors. I appreciate the intentionality of the team and the magazine's culture to highlight the most marginalized voices among us, and uplifting the wonderful and whimsical tales that inevitably arise from this structure

With that said, I am so pleased to bring to you the *Baffling Year One* anthology. When I joined the team last December, I had no idea I'd be lucky enough to bring this collection forth to you, to be perpetually blown away by the stories we've highlighted between these pages and others that continue to vie for my attention. I am so proud of what we have put together and privileged to sign my name to part of it. Thank you for joining us in this journey. Happy Reading!

Gabriella "G" Etoniru, Assistant Editor
September 2021

WHEN I ASKED my colleagues to send in their editor's notes, I expected that we'd be a month or two from publication, but time is fickle quality to it, so here we are nearly a year later. Flash fiction has been a balm to me in this moment. When a novel or even a short story feels impossible to tackle, flash fiction can offer up a tiny world, trapped in amber.

Editing a magazine is a great privilege; nothing has improved my own writing so much as reading our submissions and working with the authors we have the great fortune to publish. Publishing a magazine is also entering into a conversation—sharing the words that have sparked feeling, provoked imagination. We're so grateful that these words have found their way to us and that we've been able to bring them into the discussion.

Creative endeavors are always the sweeter with fine co-conspirators; Craig and Gabriella have been the finest of such. We've also been graced with art (covers and logos alike) from some incredible artists: Robin Ha, Mod Darkmoon, Matthew Spencer, Sajan Rai, Savanna Meyer, Nate Tazewell and Molk Tae. *Baffling* has been a strange creature to emerge during a dark time, and I couldn't have done it without all of you.

I'm also endlessly grateful to our supporters on Patreon. *Baffling* has been able to grow solely due to the generosity of these patrons. Every dollar goes directly to publishing more queer speculative fiction. Find us at patreon.com/neonhemlock if you'd like to become part of that.

Whether you are already a *Baffling* stalwart or a reader finding us for the first time in this anthology, welcome to these pages. I find you find something strange and wonderful inside.

dave ring, Co-Editor
May 2022

MERIDA, YUCATAN: 2060

JEWELLE GOMEZ

GILDA MOVED THROUGH the night air—quick and soft as a scent on the wind. She slowed her preternatural speed so she might take in the landscape around her; maybe for the final time. Here in the desert, just north of what had been the border between the United States and Mexico, lie the ruins of what had once been a domineering wall.

The combination of monumental cruelty, mundane carelessness, deliberate poisoning, a revolt against scientific principles, diseases, and war had turned this area and their planet into a wasteland. The polluted air and chemically-infused water had reduced life expectancy to fewer than 60 years for most of the population, especially the poor. The planet barely gasped out its last breaths for the tiny pockets of humanity who defied authority and refused to escape to outer world colonies. Known as the Blue Marble Group, they insisted there was a way to reseed and restart the earth if corporate control could be broken.

Exorbitant fees had been paid and a ship was waiting. Gilda could feel Effie, her lover, pulling her south to the

place where they were meant to launch into a new world,
leaving the decaying corpse of this one behind. Doubts
wafted through Gilda's mind, but still she moved on. Until
it was her time to make an exchange for the blood that
gave her strength and long life, she would remain invisible
to the rare few out on the road.

When she reached the edge of what had once been a
small village, she sensed someone ahead in the darkness.
She moved more slowly, wary of encountering a Hunter,
who might try to capture her and deliver her to a wealthy
patron. Gilda would not relish being slowly drained and
having her blood transfused to lengthen another's life.

At the moment she recognized the stealthy movement
of that Hunter, another one, much closer, leapt from his
cloaking shadow, his gloved hand raised. In it—a soft,
innocent looking pad that could deliver, on contact, a
paralyzing toxin. One that would enable him to deliver
Gilda to a buyer.

Gilda's memory circled her head like projections
whirling in the air. Hiding from a slave catcher 300 years
in the past still seared her. The putrid heat of triumph
and lust had risen around that barn as he'd towered over
her. She'd seen enough lashes on the backs of others to
feel them on her own flesh as she laid in a pile of hay,
clutching a stolen rusty knife.

Rage had thrust her forward from the hay, stiffening
her arm as she plunged the knife into his soft belly. Seeing
his blood, red and rich as her own, had startled her.
Somehow, he'd only seemed human once his humanity
was ebbing away.

Gilda blinked hard, returning to the danger closing
in on her. Electricity flowed through her body, an
unstoppable current, sparked by the memory of that past
pursuit and the stink of greed from this Hunter.

Gilda turned at the last moment and struck out with
her foot in a clean move Bird would have applauded.

She downed him smoothly without breaking his neck or his back. When she took his blood, she sensed the methamphetamine he'd used to sharpen his prowess. *Clearly not enough*, Gilda thought. She considered what she could leave him in exchange for the gift of his blood. She flooded his mind with the joy of building, of planting, and a memory she had of the Painted Desert. Perhaps these might set him on a new path.

Gilda turned toward Merida again, thinking of the fragrant roses that had once grown there. She felt Effie almost near, which sent a shiver of desire through her entire body. Soon they would lie together, wrapped in their home soil and each other.

In her head, Gilda heard Bird's voice from long ago. "The despoilers have tried to steal everything from us through the centuries. The Lakota can not abandon the land again."

"My people were dragged here in chains. Perhaps I can not have the same love for this land as you do," Gilda had responded.

"Generations of your blood has fed this soil," Bird had replied softly. "Would you leave your ancestors behind?"

Gilda had no answer for Bird back then.

With Bird's voice in her mind, Gilda left all memory of the Hunter behind except for the pictures she'd planted in his head. Suddenly, the thought of never seeing the Painted Desert again was heartbreaking.

I have the blood of many in my veins, she thought, *their blood racing to my heart and washing over my brain.* She focused inward and felt Bird touching her, beckoning her to remain and fight for the land.

Stay? Fight? The questions burrowed into Gilda's mind and she began to reason out how she would explain to Effie there could be a new way: Not running, but staying. Battling for renewal of the earth, rescuing it from its captors. This time she really understood Bird's words and knew what she'd say to Effie. One of the primary precepts of their family: *We take blood, not life, and leave something in exchange.* They'd all consumed the blood of humanity for centuries, now they must give back. Now they had to return the dreams to the soil of earth, purging out the poisons that were doing their murderous work.

As she decided not to leave, Gilda thought of the Blue Marble Group. She knew that it would be no simple task to reclaim what had been stolen and violated. It would take uncountable time to route out the ancient evils that had infected those who'd ascended to power and those beneath them who still supported corruption. Power was impossible to resist.

Healing had always been women's work, Gilda thought. She couldn't imagine how many years, decades, centuries it might take to turn the tide of history, to make the earth flower again. But Gilda smiled. She and Effie and her family possessed as much time as was needed.

From the Deep the Music Rises

Izzy Wasserstein

ANA IS ALONE in the Deep when she hears the music. It's a pop song of longing for Old Terra, barely audible. She whips her head around, the lights of her exo-suit pushing ineffectually into the dark. There's nothing. No one.

For the first time in weeks, the first time since she's been working alone, she unmutes her comms.

"Keep music off the line," she demands. "I'm trying to work."

There's a long pause, longer even than it takes for the comms to cut through the Deep's time dilation.

"There's nothing on the line." Kelv's voice is tense. It's been a frequent intrusion on her long silence, both here and on the surface. He still sets a third place at their table, talks into Ana's wordlessness. The music plays on behind his words, soft and insistent. Ana recognizes the songs only through impromptu acapella. Through Prin.

"Forget it," she sets to work. Space and time work strangely in the Deep, its rules a puzzle for physicists, xenobiologists. Ana operates on instinct, using the small changes in pressure and temperature to avoid the displacement of a Leviathan, or the body-wracking presence of warp fish.

The music plays on, this time a song about youth, drugs and the lure of the unknown. Ana finds what she's looking for, the swaying lattices of netweed, their pods heavy with Deep Pearls and their ultra-valuable exotic matter.

"Maybe...you should come back up," Kelv says. Ana doesn't respond. If she comes up, he'll tell management she's cracking, and they'll make her take on a new partner. Never again.

She moves deliberately, watching for deadly tangles of netweed. She's always been good at her job, always been able to hyper-focus, even when her comms had been full of Prin's singing, high-pitched, crystal-sharp. Now she struggles, her hands shake.

A new song starts. She fumbles, drops a Pearl, its luminescent surface falling slowly, just out of reach. She almost lunges for it, then catches herself. A half-meter further and she'd have been caught in the netweed, pulled down and down into the darkest depths. The memory of Prin comes unbidden, her struggling body yanked down--

Ana's desperate to avoid the memory, but the music. Won't. Stop. It's "Drawn Back 2U," the song Prin had been singing at the last. Ana swallows back vomit, imagines letting herself be taken.

Something is with her. The hairs on her arms stand straight. She freezes. Just in time. A school of Rippers swims past, eyeless, needle-toothed, their motion-sensing ridges fluttering in the current.

"Ana, your heart rate's spiking," Kelv says, urgent. Ana has no choice but to stay silent. The Rippers pass within a meter of her. Kelv's voice grows more panicked.

Finally the school disappears into the depths. "Rippers," she whispers. "Gone now."

She's alone. The music drifts up to her. She returns to

her harvest, but Kelv's still speaking, his voice cracking: "Come up, Ana. Please, come up. I can't lose you, too."

His words are barely audible against the fragile notes rising from the Deep, calling her down, urging her to join them. Her silence stretches.

The music will always be there, waiting, calling to her. Beckoning.

"I'm coming up," Ana says at last. She follows Kelv's voice to the surface.

Cellars, Caskets & Closets

Maxwell I. Gold

Inside a twisted rhizome of mutilated greyspaces through cellar doors, dripping with speckled layers of teal plaster and pulp, the awful smell of paint and wood scratched my nostrils as I lost my goddamn mind. It happened all the time, finding myself trapped in the gutted ramparts of my consciousness, stranded atop a tower in the mountainous webs of brain matter and bile with no way out. No one to talk to, no kind or familiar voices to console me. Only dark and distant shadows, vibrating against my ears. Through petrified wood doors, where rusty hinges swayed in the stale air, I caught passing glances of a world that could be, not this place layered in false judgments and licentious thoughts of insincerity.

In cyanide dreams, I pulled a casket of iron and marble from cellar to cellar, tower to tower, voices chasing me inside my head, afraid to open the metal box, wanting to destroy it. They weren't monstrous corporeal things wrought by some galactic calamity or creatures borne of stardust, no, it was worse. The banality of the things that gnawed at the foundations of my mind laughed in tones of abject sadness; towering over me in immensities of black silence and subjective uselessness, with bodies constructed in liquescent mirrors and thoraxes of neon and metal. Inhuman and relentless, were the only feelings I had to describe shrill cackles as I attempted to blot out the pounding noises. Behind me, I could feel the lucidity of dreams wither under the greyness and grandeur as the Mirrored Ones began to grind their iron teeth into the fabric of my thoughts, triturating them into dust.

I ran, heaving the casket as the laughter grew in tidal waves of metallic sounds, their rusty thoraxes screeching as they tromped closer attempting to snatch the box, voices exhaling in a crescendo of wanton putrid pragmatic corrosion, eroding my will. Towers, cellars, all swallowed into the wading abysm of mirrored silence, where dark shadowy fingers grasped the edge of the casket. The laughter soon shifted from a raucous symphony to howling moans; my head throbbing, sinuses clogged with the familiar scent of paint and wood as the casket disappeared, where inside a twisted rhizome of mutilated greyspaces through cellar doors, dripping with speckled layers of teal plaster and pulp, I lost my goddamn mind.

VELVET

NINO CIPRI

THE SUBURB WAS called Deer Meadows, and it was a truer name than most developments. Finn Foulbec had grown up with the deer, could always spot the shape and silhouette of the small herd watching from someone's backyard or the treeline between two properties. If Finn woke up fussing before dawn, Mr. Foulbec strapped him into his car seat and hit the road, making turns at random through the neighborhood until Finn quieted down and slept. Finn, unbidden, often still rose at the same time as his father, and together they took an early-morning drive around the neighborhood. The smell of Mr. Foulbec's coffee filled the interior of the car, and they listened to classic country music turned low, songs that invoked the kind of loneliness that can only happen under wide-open Western skies or secretive Appalachian hollers. Nobody sang country songs about suburbs, where the sky was circumspect and you could see in everybody's windows at night.

Then again, the neighborhood looked strange during those early morning drives, especially in the winter; alien and hard to recognize. The engine, the heat, the music,

the smells of coffee and his father's aftershave provided
only a provisional safety. Finn was never more aware of
it than when the car came to a slow halt as the herd of
deer crossed the street, eyes glowing in the headlights.
When it was cold like this, in the barren weeks of January,
steam rose from the deer's flanks, curling into the icy air.
Sometimes the deer would stop and stare at the car; Mr.
Foulbec said that some prey animals couldn't help but be
entranced by headlights, even as they're speeding down
on them. It hypnotizes them. When that happened, Mr.
Foulbec would blast the horn at the animals, startling
them into an inelegant dash to the other side of the road.

He'd gone for a drive with his father earlier in the week,
but the whole encounter had been off from the start. Finn
had woken up a few minutes early and stumbled to the
bathroom to pee, not noticing the light pooling beneath it.
His father had been in the bathroom, already undressed
and waiting for the water to heat up. It was like opening
the door to a stranger, hairy and flushed, the smell of him
musty from sleep, a monster half-obscured by the steam.
His face was blotchy red beneath the stubble, and there
were pink creases tucked beneath the wide swell of pale
belly, where the elastic of his underwear had pinched the
skin. He opened his mouth, but before he could speak,
Finn stumbled back out of the bathroom, pulling the door
shut behind him.

Later, when they encountered the herd, one of the stags
had been shedding the velvet from his antlers. It had hung
in strips nearly to the stag's eyes, and the sight of them
had made Finn shudder in revulsion. The drive had been
ruined.

Finn got out of bed and crossed to the window. They
never decided beforehand that they would take a sunrise
shift drive. It either happened or it didn't; today, he woke
up just a little too late. Outside, Mr. Foulbec went through
a routine so habitual Finn could shut his eyes and envision

every step: unlock the doors, set the thermos on the roof, toss his bag in the back seat, put the thermos in the drink holder, sit down, turn on the car, switch the radio from news to the country station, back down the driveway with one big hand braced on the passenger side headrest. Finn blinked his eyes open as the sounds of the engine faded, and was left with a view of the woods beyond their front yard. Mrs. Foulbec never had to tell Finn not to go into the woods—he avoided them on his own. Now their profile carved out a more solid darkness into the surrounding night; dark like an absence, like a hole in the world. It held Finn's eyes for a while until he was able to turn away, let the curtain fall, and get back into bed.

When Finn found himself in the woods, he assumed it was a dream. He stood barefoot on the cold, hard ground, with the grass crunching frost beneath him. The icy wind cut right through the thin cloth of his pajamas, but the cold felt strangely good, even as his skin broke out in gooseflesh.

A stag stood only a dozen feet away from him. Its rack of antlers carried bloody strips of velvet, a dangling ruin of shredded flesh. The stag took no notice of Finn and stepped closer to one of the nearby pines, rubbing its antlers against the bark. The dull clacking of it made Finn think of bones rattling together. What kind of dream was this, where he could so clearly feel the cold, could smell the wild musk rising from the deer's haunches? Something uneasy stirred in Finn's stomach, and he took a dazed step forward. The stag froze, turning until it caught Finn full in its glare.

Finn took another step back, ducking behind a tree. He uttered a soft, disgusted cry as something wet brushed his hand and wrist; there was a strip of bloody velvet clinging to his skin.

The stag huffed and stamped a foot, and Finn pressed his face against the tree.

Wake up, he thought. *Wake up in your warm room to Mom calling your name. Wake up to the smell of her milky tea and toast, with the ghost of Dad's coffee still lingering in the air. Wake up to a real morning.*

Finn didn't wake up, not then and not at the eerie, guttural bawl coming from another corner of the woods. The cry caught the stag's attention, and it wandered off, huffing aggressively. Finn waited until he was sure it had gone, and then limped home on feet gone numb from the cold. He could barely turn the handle of the front door to his house; his fingers were pale blue.

Finn was so cold that all he could think to do was get in the shower. The hot water hit his filthy feet like a rain of knives, peeling off his skin. He muffled his cries until the heat finally soaked into him. He was washing the dirt and pine pitch from his feet when he saw it; the long strip of velvet had stuck to him back in the woods. It seemed diminished here in his house, with most of the blood washed away, the flesh clean and sterile. He picked the strip up off the shower floor—it was slippery at first, he had to pinch it between his fingernails. He stayed in the hot water for another twenty minutes, running the velvet between his fingers, against the skin of his inner wrist, his chin, his cheeks, and finally, stringing it around his neck. When he finally got out of the shower, he wiped the condensation off the mirror to look at himself, at the pink-and-gray strip of velvet and blood vessels that he'd knotted tight against his throat.

Finn stared until the mirror fogged over again, hiding him from sight.

BIRDS ARE TRYING TO REINVENT YOUR HEART

JENNIFER MACE

BIRDS ARE TRYING to reinvent your heart.

They have braided strands of kelp around a clam shell, gritty and dank with sand. As it dries, salt crystallizes and rimes the seams. It is a captured moment of the sea, a fist-sized prayer to time and tide. If you lift it to your ear, it sighs with the voice of the cliffs; to your mouth, and the taste of ocean may numb your lips like the tears of a thousand lovers.

But it is not a heart.

A heart is a carbuncle knot, a cancerous mass of grief around which your ribs have seized. A heart is a siphon to dread, to guilt, to every spear and lance the world would pin you by. A heart is a wound.

They try nonetheless, wheeling and screaming the rage that stops your tongue. Gulls rip the silvery flesh from sardines and weave their pliant bones into a net. Shy plovers fill it with seeds stripped from the ferns of the cliffs, and it rattles in your ear like the shaking of reeds in the wind. When you clench your fist, it crumbles as easy as sand.

A heart is fragile.

†

A HEART MIGHT be coaxed open by a penitent who comes to you from the shattered cliff-top villages and lays herself at your feet, her clothes still heavy with the soot of your wrath. It might beat faster when you raise her up, though she flinches at your divinity, her skin like the rasp of dune grass against your hands, her eyes as trusting as a seal's. When she sleeps in the shade of your cliffs as the moon fades and is reborn, and again, and again—a heart might be laid bare by the way the salt waves roughen her feet as she greets you in the spilled fire of dawn.

You show it to her, then. Take her hand in yours. Guide her beneath the water to caves that only exist in the shuddering moments when low tide aches to rise again. Pearls scatter beneath your feet, your backs, the tribute of a thousand thousand oysters spread in an irreverent iridescent bed.

And as you lie there, replete, salt creeping ever nearer to your toes, she pulls her conch-carved blade from the tangled discards of her garments and slips it sweetly into your breast. Her eyes are still soft as moonlight. Her hands tremble.

You kill her, of course. Mortals are even more fragile than hearts.

†

PELICANS BRING YOU strange crab casings filled with shredded leaves of dulse and sargassum. A cormorant drops the dead spines of an urchin at your feet, flesh pecked away and replaced with the scraggling grey feathers of childhood. The auks and puffins have gathered a dozen perfect quartz pebbles and wrapped them in the glistening flesh of a jellyfish, bulbous as a sea cucumber trembling in the sun.

You crush them all. Beneath your feet, between your hands, with the ice of your breath and the stone of your teeth. They are all wrong. They cannot fix you.

The screaming gulf of your fury has ripped a storm from the heavens. It drives the waves against the tide, tears forests from the ocean floor and churns the air into an incoherent mass of feathers.

You pluck a petrel from the sky. Consider it. Inhale its frantic rolling eye, the oil of its back, the fluttering heaving bewilderment of its breast. The thudding of its tiny, tiny heart.

It passes through your lips as easy as the sea cuts down a cliff. You catch another. Another. Another. They pulse beneath your ribcage like sunlight through ten feet of water, weak as hatchlings straining against the shell.

Yes. It is a start.

Your gaze turns to the clifftops, where the first smoke of morning has begun to stain your sky the grotesque yellow-grey of sickened cod-flesh. To the sticky roar of mortal blood pounding through infidel veins.

You have become distracted. You have allowed yourself to be appeased, by soft skin and softer touch.

No more.

An army of curved beaks and fierce claws at your back, the cree of osprey and albatross ringing through the air, you press your fingers into the cliff face and begin the climb.

WHY WE MAKE MONSTERS

REM WIGMORE

H AL KNEW WHERE Crown would be the second they
saw the news. The woman on TV had fear-wide
eyes and a steady voice, but Hal could only look
at the monster behind her. A mouldering wreck as tall as
a building, heaped up on the shoreline like a continent's
worth of plastic bags. Rotting blubber folded over sharp
curves of bone, like a whale, but too many limbs and too
many eyes.

Hal ran the whole way despite the rain. It wasn't far.
Crown had wanted to live close to the ocean.

The journalist was still wrapping up her report when
they got there. "…there is a giant, rotting corpse off the
Bay," she said. "And nobody knows what it is."

Not quite nobody.

Crown of Thorns stood by the hastily-erected security
cordon, exactly where Hal knew she'd be. Her long hair
was pushed back from her face, eyes bright as she admired
her creation. Hal's spitfire lover, transformed into a mad
scientist out of the old films.

Hal took her arm. "This is a step up from mice with six
legs."

She smiled at them, then turned back to the corpse with a sigh. "Isn't it beautiful?"

Hal looked up at the hulking carcass, a deflated, rubbery tower of death. It was hard to see beauty in the rot. "Was it ever alive, or did you design it as a dramatic corpse?"

Crown's gaze dropped. "I couldn't manage to get its body plan sustainable."

Hal squeezed her arm but let go before they squeezed too tight. "What the hell was your plan? Now it just sits there, rotting pollution into the sea?"

Crown shook her head. "It's biodegradable," she said.

Hal stepped in front of her, forcing her to meet their eyes. "Crown of Thorns Jones!" they growled. "Take this seriously."

She did look at them properly now.. A shadow of what might be regret passed over her face. About as close to regret as this monster was to a whale. "I didn't know it would bother you, Halifax."

Hal stepped back to look at the carcass instead of her. Thankfully, the beast's huge eyes were all closed, no gaunt sockets to haunt Hal's dreams. Fleshy bulbs dangled from its jaw and bobbed in the water. Once-blue skin was greyed over with rot. The spine and six flippers were dotted with globs of more translucent flesh, jelly-like, that glowed a soft and slowly fading red.

Just last night everything had still been perfect. Hal had cooked dinner and gotten the balance of spices wrong like always. Crown had laughed and said she'd be happy to eat Hal's salty spaghetti forever. Said 'forever' like she meant it. And all this time she'd been keeping a secret the size of a leviathan.

Crown's voice went serious. "This will make them pay attention to the health of the ocean if anything does." She waved up at her genetically engineered edifice. "Something like this rising up? People will finally ask questions about the oxygen levels, clean out the waste—"

"Is this the whole reason we moved to the coast?" Hal said in a voice that wavered. "Why you moved in with me at all?"

Crown looked at them mutely and took their hand. Rain fell on the beast's sloping sides, sirens wailing as the city tried to decide what kind of emergency this even was.

"You were the other reason," she said.

Hal tilted their face up toward the rain and the dead monster Crown built. Perhaps buried in that corpseflesh there was a tiny seed of life, doomed genes spelling out hope. A thin hope, but with her hand in theirs, they could believe it.

SONSKINS

DARE SEGUN FALOWO

I.

ON A NIGHT of open flight, when healers take on the skins of their familiars to battle sickness, we stand rigid over our catatonic sons.

Our special peppersoup has barely dried off their lips.

II.

BEFORE THIS NIGHT, we peer into their dreams, through crisp dense hair. They dream of palaces for us, helicopters with blades of gold spinning, burning, cradling us in the noon above city heat, trips to the World's Wonders with their dead fathers kissing our cheek in the sun-decayed CANON square after, reams of overwrought handmade fabric in cool tones, spilling pearls, diamonds, sequins, stained with a drop of the weaver's blood as a gift, they dream of palaces again, of dogs splashing in fountain and barking the moon to fullness, of obedient house girls willing to suck on our split fingers and take over the chopping of the ugwu and the onions, the frying of the chicken and the pepperfish, the cooking of a perfect pot of jollof.

Our sons dream of saving us from this desolation in
which we sit like stubborn mules in mud. They wish to
erase the agony that their births and their nurturing have
inscribed on our faces, and yet, their dreams are empty of
wives.

III.

IN THESE DREAMS that we gaze into beneath the scalps
of our sons, we find them after wading through their
motherdreams, hiding in the grove. Apples surround
their feet as they grasp onto each other, naked except for
tattered wrappers, rasping beneath their low moans.

There is a beast devouring our sons, under leaves
fading away into gold.

Their wet skins glisten in that light of netherworlds.
We have no body so he can't see our faces collapse as we
behold his sin. His dream falls to tatters, corroded by our
silent shout. He doesn't let go of his beast until he startles
awake, and in the slowness of his eyelids drifting back to
sleep, taking him back to his grove of beastly desire, he
wonders why the room smells of hot anointing oil.

IV.

SO, ON THIS night when the very air seems to bristle with
the nagual, we take off our sons' skins.

As we peel off the furred slabs of pumpkin yellow,
coal black, and cocoa, we watch the bark infusion in the
peppersoup bind the ends of their nerves in tufts of muted
lime fire. We slip off the long gloves of their arms, the
trousers of their lower body, the breastplates of their torso
and the masks of their heads.

Our sons are bare, glistening, squirming things. Their
nerves burn in lightning paths under the exposed pink-
red-cream bruise of their subdermis. We cover them with
a blanket of bitter leaves and step into the heat of their
fresh skin.

V.

Now, we remember the names of the men that the Beast used to lure our sons and we hunt. On this night of open flight, the air aids our parting of space to slip through shortcuts, to find them in their rooms asleep or eating, wrapped around other men, kissing their oblivious wives.

Our sons have been busy. The Beasts have a network spanning everywhere. They touch everything with their filth, their sticky desires, their abominations of family and love. They think we are our sons when we walk out of their walls into their homes.

Some of them, the ones who live alone, soften immediately, running over to kiss us rough or soft. They palm our bodies and try to draw heat, then they look into our eyes as our fists find their throats.

Oh! The rush of breath's struggle to be free, and our insistence that it not be, that it be quiet, fuels our sonskins, causing heat to rise off us and we smother them.

Others are startled, waking up at midnight beside their taboo lovers, or their wives, to see the shadow of us standing bare and naked. They beg us as our son. "Why are you here now? How did you get in?" We pull them close into smeary kisses, as their wives and lovers wake. They look into our eyes and see we are not him.

We take their skins off while they are fully awake.

VI.

As this night tapers to an end, the skins loosen around our jaws and hips. Flaps start to tear up along the spine. The skins we have harvested hang over our left shoulder.

We return home, to the mats of bitter leaves under which our sons rest. We dust off the leaves, now dry and ready to crunch, and give our sons back their skins.

We know they will wake soon, hungry to find the Beast again. How futile our midnight errands seem against this force that no witch, Bible or pastor has been able to remove. A wildness! Ready to corrode the very foundations of the love that birthed them with its lust and its possession of their flesh.

The heat they seek which we can never give them. The heat of the touch of the Beast with which no woman can compare. This heat better than our platters of peppery food and our washing of their clothes, our peering into their dreams, our weaving of their futures and our birthing of them. They are incapable of resistance, incapable of sacrificing this desire for us.

We will find a way to make them see what we want. We have birthed them so they will give us glory, show us what we could not be.

Our sons stir in the thrum of the coming day. Their skins firm against their bones. We return to our empty beds and lay the taken skins over the mattress before going to sleep with smiles on our faces.

VII.

ON SOME OTHER night, not one of open flight or of the full moon, we find the girl. She walks down the street alone, her eyes say she is running from something. It is past 11pm. We steal her, as the Beast has stolen our sons, and then we execute our vision.

Our sons wake up again. We ask them of wives, marriage and children. They fumble around as usual, unable to find the courage to tell us what we already know, then end up with, "In my own time, Mama."

We smile. They are all above thirty and have lived under our skins for much longer. Their sorrows are our sorrows. Our joy is theirs. Now, we will give them happiness.

We bring in the girl, wearing the skin of our sons' kin.

Dreadful Necessity Governs All Things

Rien Gray

I T IS SAID the poet Areio started a war in six strokes of her pen.

That is not true: it was three.

I know this because Areio—Whose-Verse-Scorched-The-Earth, may she be honored now and forever—was both mentor and lover, and we debated many times in bed over the definition of a 'stroke'. She won more often than not, and thus I attest her claims.

The empire of Evenu sent a message housed in illustrious script and surrounded by a moat of meaning deep enough to drown us. After a decade of subtle aggressions, His Imperial Majesty's patience for peace—unconditional surrender—had reached its limit, and his proclamation was such:

There is no place the sun touches I do not possess. If you have chosen darkness, you will be extinguished in kind.

Perhaps that does not appear masterful in a scholar's shorthand, but in our true runes it held the divine weight of a guiding star, eternal and implacable: a light that conquers while in truth long dead.

It must have taken seasons to translate imperial letters into a runecoil; or perhaps, they forced one of our poets to do the work for them. To ply our own tongue against us speaks to violence, as if our resistance arose from a child's misunderstanding of tone.

The beauty of the coil is that alignment changes meaning—lines of connection fuse words into bastions of metaphor calling on our oldest stories. That is why the Evenusi loathe us. We are not satisfied with singular definitions; we lay with contradiction and treasure the overlap they share. What darkness they accuse us of is but the diversity of nature.

Areio's reply was thus:

She severed the sigil of I/Empire from the message with a single stroke, then drew a new line between the cusp of *sun* and the curve of *darkness*. The final movement was a fearsome scrawl, obliterating any notion of possession from the claim before her.

It translated simply: THE SUN HAS SET.

Of course, every war begins with a poet.

You think of soldiers, but soldiers are symptoms and not the cause. Name a viceroy or sovereign, and I shall point to the young mind behind him, an artist crafting turns of phrase to suit their master's ambitions. War fills our heads with blades and bullets, but before steel and lead, there is always breath and ink.

A poet sings of glory one evening, and by morning forges cough with smoke, shaping weapons to carve ideals into reality. A poet writes to her noble lover, and that noble's husband sees the verse; he plots the poet's murder, and her martyrdom sparks conflict that slaughters generations.

Yet banning poetry is no key to peace. A poem is but a path of influence, and like all paths can turn to destructive ends. One may as well forbid the tide, for poems enter and leave the soul in similar accordance with their own rhythm.

They transform the heart, even if they never leave one's lips.

Except these poems are a lesson half-learned. We have started countless wars, yet I cannot name one that our work has ended.

Here I confess that Areio did not begin the war that birthed her name of honor. Rather, the imperial poets did.

Because ours was not the first nation they swallowed, and when victors find their hungers unsated, they turn to the pen. They drown their atrocities in prose and smother them in paper. They write heart-stirring poems to teach our youth that war is the only way, luring them with verse like songbirds to a barbed net.

They must justify their victory and the source of their power, time and again. They are desperate to be seen, smashing the mirrors of others until they are the only ones reflected. And they succeed, because we fear to interrupt their words, no matter how destructive.

Of course we protest. We write new lyrics for new philosophies. We soothe warriors with song when they come home shattered, or whisper last hymns over the ashes that return in their place. We demand better futures in infinite structures, both classic and experimental.

Yet none of that stopped Evenusi soldiers from dragging Areio—Whose-Verse-Scorched-The-Earth, I loved her so much—by her hair from the house we shared, breaking her hands, and cutting off her head.

If my poem of grief had any effect, it was only to amuse them.

Thus the only path ahead is a new medium: not in means, but material.

This poem is written through the body. Imagine the arrangement of your limbs before a cavalcade of horsemen ten thousand astride, blood-frothed and trample-eager. You cannot stand aside, because the weapons in their hands are elegies for our children, our sick, our poor.

You must hold the poem in your flesh because they will
take everything else from you. Food. Clothes. Dignity. If
they take your flesh too, you must bury it in your bones.
You must learn couplets in other tongues, for the allies we
need will spring from every shadow the Emperor has yet
to claim. Some will even rise from the empire itself, for a
nation bound by violence can never march in unison.

Memorize the meter of their epics, for the poems passed
from mouth to mouth are the first to fall. Find euphony in
their laughter, their tears, the moments of silence we learn
to share. A litany can live on in each of us, if we wish it.

I hear what others say of me: "Look at Elash Se, sharp-
boned and born with nothing, neither man nor woman.
What do they know?"

You need not listen nor obey, for I am a poet and not a
conqueror.

But I say this: the truth of the world will only change if
we change first.

That, and I am Elash Se no longer. I am Elash Who-
Wove-the-Myth, the myth that sustained unity when our
spirits threatened to fail. The historian, the mourner, the
lover who will one day join Areio in the world beyond
worlds.

A poem has yet to end a war—but I intend to write the
first.

DEADBEAT

JACOB BUDENZ

I SIT UP, gasping. His eyes, half open. Body swaddled in Egyptian cotton. Sweat. Sunlight through blinds.

"I just won second place in a speed eating contest in Berlin," I say.

"Just now?" he says. Slow blink.

"It wasn't even just a hotdog eating contest! It was all different kinds of food."

"Mm," he curls toward me. Leg over my leg.

"Aren't you proud of me? I won second."

"Mmhmm." He doesn't mean it.

I lay back on three pillows. Eyes wide. His, closed. He knows I'm not dreaming. Knows that the process of astral projection, of possessing the body of a host, is nothing to laugh at. Used to be impressed. I possess the body of the competitor least favored to win the eating contest, stuff its face. I haven't won yet, but I'm getting better.

"I know," I say. Long exhale. Didn't realize I'd been holding my breath.

"No!" he says, waving away the smoke that seeps from my nostrils. He complains about this sort of thing—the smoke, the smell of burning hair when I lose myself in thought, the summer bonfires that burn too hot when I approach—but I really do my best. He continues, "It's fine, really." He rethinks. "I mean, it's great! Second place is great, it's…"

Doesn't say: *First loser.*

"What do I say to your parents?" I say. "It's getting, I don't know. Should I be embarrassed?"

Downstairs, his mom clatters around in the kitchen. *I'm awake!* she screams through the pots. *So everyone should be awake.* Every morning. Every. Damn. Time. We. Visit.

His eyes: still closed. "I just wouldn't mention it."

"Oh," I say. "Great, thanks." *Another deadbeat demon lover leaching off my little warlock,* sings the kettle downstairs. *Can't even win an eating contest in* Berlin. I hear the coffee mugs clink against granite. Their laughter: disappointed but not surprised.

I brace myself for it. Seconds roll past. Minutes? Then, her voice from downstairs: "Boys!"

He forces his eyes open. A naked leg slips from the shelter of the bed sheets. A grumble on the way to the bathroom, something about the word "boy," about whether it applies to him on the year of his twenty-seventh birthday. His bare ass expects applause.

I spit mouthwash into the sink beside him. Gently (he's not a morning person), I say: "It's just a mom thing. I mean, she said it to both of us, and I'm…" Ageless. I shut up. We try not to talk about the mortality thing. I try for a topic change, try the real issue at hand. "What do you think I should do about, you know, the contests?" I hate making decisions. He loves making them for me. Makes him less grumpy in the morning.

"Probably take it easier on yourself? You really are getting close, you know," he says, and I'm surprised to admit that he sounds like he means it. "I think you've gotta chill out a little. You've cracked the code, but you're burnt out."

"You really think so?" Something very like relief—I can't say for sure; it's been decades—loosens sinew in my back and shoulders.

"I mean, you literally singed the edge of the pillowcase last night." He gargles toothpaste-water, spits. "Maybe try to sleep for real. Take a nap this afternoon." He looks at me from the corner of his eye. Mouth upturned. Lascivious. "Stay on this side of the planet tonight. I can make you good and hungry for something you can't eat with someone else's mouth."

He turns to me and licks his toothpaste-coated upper lip, raising one eyebrow cartoonishly. In spite of myself, I do laugh. One short burst.

"But seriously. You look like you haven't slept all month."

I consider my mug in the mirror. Dark pillows under darker eyes. All month? If only, child. It's been far, far longer than that.

EMBRACE OF MEMORY

BRIAN RAPPATTA

A WEEK AFTER the funeral, I met Dad for coffee at
Bentham's. He greeted me with a warm hug that
lasted a few beats longer than usual.

"How you holding up, kiddo?" he asked as we sat at the
table next to our regular one. A couple of hipsters were sitting
in ours. How long had it been since we'd been here last?

"Fine," I said.

"And Margot?"

She was urging me to go to therapy, which I kept
putting off with some excuse or other. "Fine."

"And Carson?"

Carson had barely known his other grandfather, so it
was no lie when I said, "Fine." I paused. "What about
you, Dad? How're you holding up?"

He swallowed. The uncharacteristic three days' worth
of white stubble on his neck couldn't quite hide how loose
the folds of his skin looked. But he mustered a smile for
my benefit. "I'm fine. Really." "Your father left something
for you." Dad reached into his jacket pocket before sliding
something across the table to me. "He recorded it before he
passed on."

It was a tactile fob. I cast a surreptitious look around the cafe to see if we'd drawn any attention. Knee-jerk reaction. Most people didn't exchange these things in crowded cafes. Margot and I were always recording tactile experiences for each other, but they were surely of a much different nature than what was on this fob.

I frowned. "What's on it?"

"It's a hug. He just...wanted you to know——"

I spared Dad the burden of completing his sentence. "A hug? He wasn't exactly a touchy-feely kind of guy. Why would he leave this for me?"

Dad shrugged. "I think...after he got sick...it wasn't so much about who he was, but more about who he'd always wanted to be."

I still hadn't taken the fob, so he slid it a bit closer. "I know you and he had your differences. Just...play it when you're ready."

†

SOME THINGS REQUIRE a bit of liquid courage. I think I'd learned that from Father. So, three days later, alone in my study at home, with a fifth of bourbon in my belly, I took the fob out of my bottom-most drawer.

I plugged the fob into the port on my computer, and placed my left palm on the tactile mat hooked into it. I took a deep breath, but paused before clicking PLAY on the pop-up menu. *It's just...data*, I told myself. That's all it was. The hardware merely manipulated sensory receptors, sending haptic feedback throughout the body to simulate the touch recorded on the fob. There was nothing real about it.

I took my palm off the tactile mat. On a whim, I dug through my old files, and found the videos from my wedding reception. That was the last occasion where my father and I had been in the same room—where all the arguments and screaming matches had fortunately taken a back seat to the celebration of the moment. After a bit of scrolling, I found the file of Father and I hugging...

Yup. It looked every bit as awkward and forced as I remembered. No memory is stronger than tactile memory.

Just get it over with. I replaced my palm on the mat, and hovered over the PLAY button. It was just data. It was just a fake hug...like all the other displays of affection from my father throughout his life. It was likely to make my skin crawl, but that was closure of a sort, too, wasn't it?

"Or," Margot had told me last night, when I'd spoken to her about the fob, "you *could* think of it as a last gesture from an imperfect man who loved you very much. Most people would give anything to have a last hug from their parents. Maybe you should hold onto that thing until you're in the right headspace to be able to play it?"

She'd always been the smart one in our relationship.

With a sigh, I clicked out of the menu and disconnected the fob from the computer. I put the fob back in the desk.

Not today.

†

AND NOT FOR the next month, either. As the funeral arrangements and condolences and thoughts and prayers receded into the haze of memory, so, too, did the tactile fob buried in my desk drawer.

Until my next business trip. After I unpacked my laptop and the accompanying mobile tactile mat, I pulled the fob from my wife out of the interior pocket of my suitcase where she always left them. Normally, in the privacy of my hotel rooms, I was eager to plug the fob into the system and see what kind of tactile treats Margot had recorded for me...

But then I remembered the fob from Father...and believe me, he was the last person I wanted to be thinking of when I closed my eyes to be think about my wife.

I packed up the whole system, put it back in my suitcase, and laid on the double bed staring up at the patterns on the hotel room ceiling.

†

Tonight.

It had been over a month since Dad had given me the fob. I sat at my desk at home with the fob plugged into the computer, and my hand on the tactile mat. I took a deep breath. I hovered over the PLAY button on my screen.

And hesitated.

I had good memories of Father, too, I reminded myself. They were hazy and indistinct, from deeper back in my childhood: the picnics that he and Dad and I'd used to have in Wainwright Park, the...the...

I wracked my brain. Surely there had to be something else. Something before the animus that had seeped in between us, as insidious and stealthy as the cancer that had taken him.

I swallowed. Playing the tactile rendering of his final hug would bring all the good memories to the fore, and banish all the negative ones to the trash bin of memory... right? Surely that was his intent in making the recording.

My fingers hovered over the PLAY button. But was it fair to supplant all those memories with something so...fake?

Finally, I summoned my courage. I pressed DELETE instead. The dialogue box asked me if I really wanted to erase all the data on the fob.

I pressed CONFIRM.

Then, I played the blank fob, and felt...nothing. My nerve receptors remained unaffected.

Yes. This was right. It felt like all our last few conversations together. If I closed my eyes, I could almost imagine he was here in the room with me.

PEAT MOSS AND OIL FOR BURNING

A.B. YOUNG

1. OPEN-BELLIED VANITY

The devil's green coat hangs on the hook by the door.

Elle installed the hook when she moved in. The landlord said she shouldn't attempt any repairs herself. The way he looked her up and down when he said it, Elle knew he didn't think women could use power tools. Her mum said, "Fuck that," and lent her a drill.

Now Elle hopes the hook is sturdy enough. She imagines the devil's coat is quite heavy. Who knows what he keeps in his pockets?

"Do you take milk in your tea?" Elle asks, glancing over her shoulder.

The devil sits at her rickety round dining table, one cloven hoof on the other knee. He's dressed in dark green flannel and tight blue jeans, his beard lush.

"Please," he says, and he bleats the 'ee.'

When she's made the tea and they're sitting across from each other, she's...nervous isn't the right word, but there's something like it sweltering in the creases of her palms. She wipes her hands on her velvet skirt under the table.

"I made you a playlist," the devil says, and syncs his phone to her bluetooth speaker without asking.

2. FOX STOMACH MID-YAWN

Elle decomposes as she falls in love.

She's functional, mostly. She can walk and talk and eat.
But all she does is lay in bed and daydream about possible
futures with the devil. Rot is inevitable.

They kiss for the first time on a tram: the devil brackets
her beside the ticket machine, says, "God, I like you," as
he leans in.

Elle's eye sockets go waxen.

They kiss for the first time in her front doorway: the
devil claims the whole space. When he grins, his teeth are
a mangled mess and Elle finds it endearing. He whispers,
as if his feelings are a secret just for her, "Can I kiss you?"

The dry skin on the back of Elle's hands splits and leaks
yellowing fluid.

The first 'I love you' happens after sex: the devil says,
"I love the noises you make." Elle hides her face in the
pillow, utters a muffled, "Thanks." He presses reverent
kisses to her shoulder. "I love you, Elle."

Her hair falls out in clumps.

3. OPEN WOUNDS

Elle only comes when she masturbates.

After they have sex, Elle always has to assure the devil
that it's normal—as long as everyone has fun, orgasm isn't
necessary.

It's not that she doesn't believe it. Feeling wanted is like
hairpin wrists, bleeding lips, sliding whiskey. Filed teeth
holding her gut together.

That's enough.

She just wishes she didn't have to make the devil feel
better about not being able to make her come—when
she's, you know, the one who didn't come.

The devil isn't bad at sex. His oral is passable, and he
holds her down when she wants him to. But he also thinks
his penis is bigger than it is. This seems closely tied to his

self-perception, so Elle doesn't tell him when, during their short stint at polyamory, the guy she dates is significantly bigger.

She also comes the second time she has sex with him. She doesn't tell the devil that either.

4. KEYS PRESSED LIKE FLOWERS BETWEEN PAGES BETWEEN PALMS

He never asks to read her stories and Elle tells herself that's okay.

He doesn't enjoy fiction, he says. He couldn't give any good feedback. It's just not his area of expertise.

But writing makes Elle shimmer.

The devil says, "It's not like I expect you to take an interest in my art." He's working on a giant canvas on the floor. The blood of small animals fills buckets around him, and he's got paints by Stuart Semple (he refuses to use Anish Kapoor; he doesn't financially support problematic men). His art pulls heavily from expressionism.

Elle doesn't really like it aesthetically. But it's *his* art, so she listens to his rants on technique, even shows him music and writing that reminds her of his work.

But he won't read her writing, or her favorite book, or watch her favorite TV shows. She has the distinct sensation of her ribcage crackling like twigs underfoot.

5. STEP FROM TREES AND INTO HEADLIGHTS

Elle and the devil are getting married.

Her mum and aunt sit in the front row. Her aunt dabs her eyes with a handkerchief. She whispers, "She looks like a cow in that dress."

Elle's cousins, an endless sprawl of sticky pre-teen children, take up all the other seats.

Ants make trails from the peonies to the wedding cake. Some of the children wiggle on creaking chairs as ants crawl up the legs of their pants.

The devil clears his throat. "I wrote my own vows."

Elle's aunt wails.

The priest says, "The groom was still writing his vows as the bride walked down the aisle."

"Marriage isn't necessary," the devil begins. "No one I know has a happy marriage."

Elle waits for more, but that seems to be all he's going to say. Her palms swelter. She says, "We agreed we were doing the classic 'to have and to hold', so I didn't write anything."

The priest scoffs. "Typical woman."

6. *FUNGI STAGNANT BETWEEN NOTCHES OF THE SPINE*

"Bears like sweet things," the devil whispers, breath hot on her ear.

The bar is loud, and Elle feels sweat leach down the backs of her knees.

He chafes a finger against her cheek. One of her eyelashes clings to his knuckle. He holds it before her lips.

She blows, wishing for the same thing she has for years: *I wish for me and the devil to live happily ever after.*

"If a bear takes a fancy to you, he'll eat you up."

7. *GASP. STUMBLE.*

In an alternate life, Elle dates a pretty girl who is nice to her.

In an alternate life, Elle lives with her mum and comes home from work every day to unwavering emotional support.

She's read all the books on her bookshelf.

She writes everyday.

Her plants don't wilt because she always remembers to water them, and her cat doesn't piss on the carpet, and when she hands her heart, whole and beating, to the devil, he holds it safely.

He holds it softly.

Sets it down in a maidenhair fern, nestled among peat moss. He puts tealights in an oil burner and the scent is like warm cotton.

8. THE OLD WOMAN SAYS, "YOU SEE? NOW I'VE GOT TWO SOULS IN PLACE OF YOUR ONE."

The divorce papers come in the mail.

Elle places them on the rickety table and makes herself a cup of tea. She has all the time in the world.

On perusal, she finds the devil has already signed, a cloven hoof print stamped in glittering green ink. Elle pulls the pen cap off with her teeth and signs where the tabs instruct.

It all feels very casual, this ending.

Elle gulps the last of her tea, then stands and glances around her kitchen.

Here's the catch: once you've married the devil, you don't get your soul back.

Vanity Among Worms

Brent Lambert

EVERY INFLUENCER SAID all the hot guys would be there
and Cletus hadn't left his house to go out in months.
Relocating to a new city hadn't been as easy as he
thought. Beautiful people and beautiful weather coupled
with a whopping heap of self-hate left much to be desired.
The fresh, reinvigorating life he sought out hadn't shown
up yet. All his new friendships felt hollow and all the ones
he'd left behind had grown in a direction he couldn't
follow.

So right about now, Cletus was willing to try anything.
Even a seedy nightclub offering up some bizarre unique
magical experience.

Honestly, he just needed to feel wanted.

The place still smelled like an old warehouse no matter
how much the nightclub pretended otherwise. They didn't
check him for any curse marks or elder relics at the door,
but Cletus imagined the bouncers had more than enough
power to put down anyone looking to cause trouble. Most
mages in this city didn't pack much of a punch anyway,
all their power turned inward to vanity. Something he
couldn't do.

Who would start trouble here anyway? The heat,
the half-naked men chiseled by vanity magic and drugs
dancing against each other, the hypnotic thrum of the
music. It was the closest he had felt to being intoxicated
since running away from Albany and Donnie.

Worms, pulsing and purple, littered the dance floor.
He looked down once and the writhing mass nearly
nauseated him so he kept his focus ahead. The crunching
against his bare feet became more tolerable the further he
ventured into the club. He breathed deeply and focused
on absorbing the secret of this place.

The pink bloom wafting from the crushed worms
emitted a feeling of euphoria. Cletus's body tingled, his
blood rushed and every touch of skin against his own
felt rapturous. The debilitating loneliness lifted and
confidence seeped into his bones. Music seduced him
into dancing with abandon. He barely felt or heard the
crunch beneath his feet. Every breath brought a new level
of sensation. Hungering for more, he went deeper into the
club's crowd. Closer to bodies and further away from the
gnawing lack of touch that came with journeying to new
places.

After one particularly deep inhalation, he locked eyes
with a necromancer—the white lipstick gave it away. He
had a nose ring that glistened almost as much as the sweat
on his lean torso; his dark brown skin that shimmered
from the little moonlight entering the warehouse. He
smiled ravenously as Cletus approached.

"You're new here aren't you?" the necromancer asked
loud enough to be barely heard over the music. His voice
made Cletus shiver. The necromancer's slender finger ran
down his chest. "I always pick out the new ones. What's
your name?"

Perpetual bliss and sensation made him feel foolish.
Swallowing hard, his blood rising even more, he fought
against his embarrassment to say, "Cletus."

"Clee—" the necromancer pushed up against him, letting him know he shared his mutual excitement and leaned into his ear, "—tus. I like it."

Cletus bit his lip to keep from groaning. "What's yours?"

"Does it matter? I'll probably be one of a dozen mages you kiss tonight. Everyone cuts loose on their first time." The necromancer's fingers lingered down by Cletus's belt buckle. "And who can blame you? The air calls for it."

Cletus wanted to kiss the necromancer right then and there. Every nerve in his body desired him. The momentary embarrassment he felt washed away and was replaced by need. He pressed his hands against the necromancer's chest.

"If you tell me your name I'll make you my only."

"I enchanted these you know," the necromancer said, bending down to pick up one of the still squirming worms and popping it into his mouth. His eyes flashed an intense purple and a smile spread across his lips. "Too potent for a first-nighter like you to eat though."

Before this moment, the thought of eating an enchanted worm would have grossed Cletus out, but now he wanted to know. "How long till I can?"

"However long you need," the necromancer said and finally kissed him. He tasted like lavender. Cletus' body was on fire. He searched the necromancer's body with no regard to who watched until he felt other hands against him. Cold hands. Impossibly cold. He pulled back from the necromancer and looked around him. The once beautiful men around him were now gray and gaunt, their faces collapsed like only the worst famine could. Cletus screamed and the necromancer's hand gripped his shoulders when he tried to back away.

"It only lasts a moment. They'll be beautiful again and so will you." The necromancer looked at him with hungry eyes. "You wanted to be wanted didn't you? They all did."

Cletus shook his head, his horror at war with the continuing effects of the worms still being crunched beneath his feet. "Are they dead?"

"Does it matter? They all came here looking for the glamour of adoration." He started to massage Cletus' shoulders. "I knew you the moment you arrived. A lonely soul who thought he could come somewhere new and escape all his crushing doubts. But cities like this are a worse curse than anything I might devise. They make you hate every inch of yourself and give you that loneliness tenfold. That's why you came here."

His panicked breaths allowed Cletus to take in more of the pink mist. He could feel himself letting go of his fear. Would staying here be so bad? The people here would desire him forever. And in turn, he would too. Was it really such a bad thing to want to be desired?

"I'll stay." Cletus leaned his head back against the necromancer's chest. "Just don't let it stop."

The music started again and all the beauty came pouring back in. Slowly, the necromancer ran his fingers through his new patron's hair. "My name is Alluros."

It was his first night. And it always would be.

ᗴARL ᑅREY

JAE STEINBACHER

I KNEW THERE was something different about Jonna the minute she walked into the cafe. I'd had so many lackluster first dates, waited so long to meet someone to fall for. The first time we kissed, it utterly consumed me.

"I love you," I told her two weeks later, the words surprising me, and my mouth filled with the taste of honey and cream spritzed with lemon.

"That happens," she said, after she'd stopped kissing me and our giddiness had ebbed.

"Really?" I asked, surprised by my disappointment. It was a novelty I wanted to be ours, and ours alone.

"Just once or twice," she assured me, taking my hand. "Nothing that lasted."

There was no reason or one cuisine behind the synesthesia. The next time I said the words, it was velvety chocolate and anise. Then scallops simmered in butter. Then the sweet flesh of roasted chestnuts.

As we went through the phases and motions of our love, she fed me a smorgasbord. Soft cheeses and flowery liqueurs. Umami and freshly baked bread. Sometimes in our passion, love was a heavy korma sauce or the juice of a grilled mushroom cap. Other times, when I held her after a bad dream, it was rose petals spun in sugar. When we woke in the mornings and I kissed her forehead, it was the yolk of an over-easy egg.

In the fervor of our early love, I told Jonna everything. The salty brine of olives after a night out, sticky rice in light miso broth when she nursed me better from the flu. Fried chicken skin rolled in cayenne when I let her tie me up. Bitter stalks of Swiss chard after our first fight.

We spent as much of our time together as we could while still getting by at work, family gatherings, and the ever more infrequent evenings with friends. I practically forgot my own bed, barely saw my roommate, knew the bus routes from her place better than mine.

I put on a few pounds, the weight of a good love, filling like blood and grease from a seared steak. I didn't tell her, but that was what I tasted after the makeup sex that left us bruised and grinning.

Any recipe can go wrong. Too much sugar; too much salt. Too much heat, or not enough. Dried out. Burnt. Putrefied.

The first time I winced after telling Jonna I loved her, she said, "What?"

I shook my head. "Just ice cream. I didn't expect the cold." Strawberry, so freezer-burnt I could taste the ice crystals.

Then it was chalky antacids. A tough cut of sushi. Wilting spinach. Overdone pasta.

I began sleeping at home more, showing up to work early once again. My friends were happy to see me out. My parents asked why I didn't bring Jonna to Mom's birthday.

"She's not feeling well," I told them. A lie instead of, *We're having a rough time.*

We kept trying. There were still moments of crisp apples, hearty stews, sweet nightcaps. But more and more, love rotted on my tongue. I lost my appetite, lost weight, lost my desires—all of them, not just for Jonna. Unwilling to swallow another curdled *I love you*, I stopped saying those words altogether.

"This isn't working, and neither of us can fix it," Jonna told me. It was a cold day after a week apart, and she'd finally invited me back to her place again. We held each other and cried, broken and relieved at the same time.

When I left, she told me, "I still love you."

"I love you too." I was hesitant, but there was no decay. Just a soft note of Earl Grey tea.

I went home to unpack the things I'd left at her place. To hibernate and heal through the cold months.

Half a year later, it was late spring. My roommate and I had been cleaning, tossing out all the fouled food in the fridge, making space for new things. I didn't know if I was ready for a love like Jonna's again. And maybe that was for the best.

One April afternoon, I held a new lover's hand as we wandered through their neighborhood, stopping to admire the tulips that had shot up in every color.

"I love you," I said, twining my fingers in theirs, breathless and a little afraid. I waited. And tasted only saliva and a freshness in the still-chilly air.

BANDIT, REAPER, YOURS

JEN BROWN

O NE HARDLY EXPECTS to be bested by a boutique. Especially not by some spongy wooden hovel, swollen from storms pummeling the Citadel's bay. Yet, the reaper Retwa is unmade, stripped like fresh carrion, every time she spots it.

Ahead, Haroux's House of Celestial Fashion sits, gauzed by gas lamps streaking the dawn. A frequent customer, Retwa has visited for all manner of delights: gallant gowns, fashionable robes, her lover's kiss.

But nothing good ever lasts.

I'll break her quickly, she thinks; Retwa shoves its loamy door open with broad shoulders, blinking back tears. It gives easily, unaware of the carnage she's come to commit, and Retwa stumbles—heart pounding—into the abyss.

Darkness shrouds the shop.

Were she a fool, or an optimist, she'd *hope*, she'd pray, that her mark had fled. Instead, she peers past Haroux's overly frilled blouses, past colorless trousers and dour hats to find her target—smirking at her, no less!—amid the shadows.

"Morning, Bandit."

Y'andi, Haroux's talented apprentice, whose every
garment screams *Out of my way, I've bones to break and souls
to sever*, regards her from the tailor's platform, voice warm
around Retwa's codename.

"Why are you still here?" Despite her training, Retwa
approaches, trembling from lace gloves to sandaled feet.
"You knew I was coming."

"Oh, Bandit. Like you, I've a job to finish." Brazen,
Y'andi meets her halfway. "Where else would I be?"

*Telling Haroux that Citadel reapers are onto him; telling
him that his secrets threaten your life.* Instead, she rasps:
"Running."

Y'andi crowds her, purring. "And give your Cadre,
or Archlorist, or whoever paid you, the satisfaction?"
Stretching, she kisses Retwa, flutter-soft, then harder,
pulling groans from them both. "Never."

Retwa saw this coming. A spy and an assassin, with
competing employers, each fevered touch enjoyed only on
stolen time. They'd burned bright and hard; why gawk at
the cinders now?

Still, she reels and painstakingly bolts the door.

"By order of the Imperial Reaper Cadre, I'm bone-
bound to hold you accountable." Feeling stripped from her
skin, Retwa continues, monotone. "Do you deny stealing
our cull-cards for Haroux's underground gossip trade?
Selling them to our targets, and thus impeding our work?"

"No."

"Did you pay another reaper to bone-bury knowledge
of Haroux's whereabouts within yourself?"

"Maybe."

Retwa frowns. "If you didn't—will you just tell me
where he is?"

"Ask nicely, and I might."

"...*Please*."

Twisting brown lips, Y'andi pantomimes thinking.
"Nah. I'd rather steal the cull-cards you're carrying now—

and fit you for that suit you ordered." She winks. "Shall we?"

Dread-filled, Retwa follows Y'andi to the tailor's stand, exchanging her reaper's robes for an ebon suit of Y'andi's making—glamorous tulle trousers, and a shimmering blazer. In the dressing mirrors, she watches Y'andi's reflection, wiry and wry-mouthed, pin and prod at her.

"If you've buried memories pertaining to Haroux, I've been ordered to shatter bones." Retwa pauses, throat thick. "I'll have to break you for them, Y'an."

Y'andi claps. "*Oh*, I've outdone myself, Bandit. Everything fits you perfectly." She searches Retwa's discarded robes like old times. "Don't reapers put bones back together, once they're done? Unless you're here to *completely* sever me, in which case, break away. Apparently, soul-stuff dribbles right out."

"I'm not here for that," Retwa says. "Are you even listening?"

"Mm…" Y'andi withdraws the cull-cards naming Retwa's latest targets—a vastmage spy, close to the Emperor; a Lorist, embezzling constellation tithes—and studies them, nose wrinkled. "Hasn't been much worth listening *to*, yet."

"For fuck's sake, Y'an—" Retwa snarls. "Haroux made you steal *excessively*, while I kept them off your trail. Then, he left the moment my Cadre grew suspicious—exposing you both! Why shield him now?"

"Because it challenges you." Y'andi says, spittle and fear hissing her words. "To choose us over your Cadre."

Us. The word hangs there, assaulting Retwa's dry mouth. Then, in a motion that's so *her* it makes Retwa snort, Y'andi pockets the cull-cards.

"I'm done making Haroux rich. I want my own fashion house—my own gossip networks—far from here." She grins, stretching the mole atop her lips. "And I want you with me."

Retwa staggers, hands sweating. "You're mad."

"I'm insistent. You know what else I want? Your real name, Bandit. Not that moniker you wall yourself behind."

"I-I'd be a fool to—"

"True fools would leave. This morning. Right now." Removing her apron, Y'andi discards fabric shears and pincushions, stripping herself of station and store. "Come away with me."

Forty-seven seconds elapse—almost silent, if it weren't for clanging streetcars bearing denizens to portside dock jobs and vastmages toward hillside shrines. Forty-seven numb footed, gape-mouthed seconds, wherein Retwa toes a tantalizing precipice.

A chasm for fools.

She grimaces. "You want all of me, Y'an? I'm no pious figure, like vastmages from old starlore. I'd leave broken sternums and severed souls wherever we went. We'd always be running."

"And fucking." Y'andi laughs, sauntering close. "Thieving for coin. Reaping whenever we damn well please—well, you'd reap, anyway. We'd be *living*, Bandit." She seizes Retwa, infectiously giddy, making Retwa shiver in return. "We'd make our own way, Haroux and your cadre be damned."

Outside, footsteps pad. Muffled, but close. Pulling away, Retwa sighs, readying herself for a different problem looming just out of sight. "Perhaps…*after* I've dealt with my colleagues."

Behind them, the door rattles without wind to speak of.

"Get back."

Y'andi retreats, moments before an imperial reaper, black-masked and grim-mouthed, barrels inside. *Interesting.* She'd counted two tailing her here.

"Reaper!" The unfamiliar figure challenges, High Imperium pristine. "We were right to doubt your loyalties."

Retwa blinks, unspooling herself, a reaper's cleaving between mind and body. She draws tendrils of soul, opaque and onyx, from her phalanxes until her fingers are cloudy with pitch.

"Spot on," Retwa slurs, unable to feel her teeth. "Now, shall we?"

Her colleague unfurls, too. They clash and dodge and topple Haroux's poor mannequins. Striking out, gloves abandoned, souls seeking skin.

They could shoot one another—most reapers carry stilettos for botched culls. But the cadre has standards. Retwa refuses to shirk them now. The rules demand she cling to her body, sidestepping their sloppy blows, and wrap sweating palms around her colleague's eyes.

That she surge her soul beneath skin and sclera, spider their frontal bone, soul crystallizing between its collagen—and shatter it.

Gurgling, her colleague thuds, feathery soul drifting up and through the rafters. Retwa sways into waiting arms.

"That was too easy," Y'andi says, cradling her. "They'll send others."

"Oh yes. There's one outside, watching now." Retwa smiles. "But we'll be long gone before they've reported us…living, and, hm—fucking by then?"

Y'andi responds with a kiss, teeth-heavy and laugh-tinged, smoothing Retwa's now-mussed suit. "Obviously. But first, what do I call the Bandit who beguiled me this year?"

Sunlight streams through the streaked storefront, highlighting the maelstrom: mannequins, upended; a body, splayed and husked. Centering it, Retwa sprawls, unscathed and unbroken.

"Retwa, for every day. Reaper, sometimes. Bandit, if you're feeling frisky." She smiles. "But whatever I am, I'm yours, Y'an. I'm all yours."

A Lamentation, While Full

M.L. Krishnan

Matriarch.

Mappilai Samba, the bridegroom's rice, soaked in water. Ground with a slurry of liquid between two stones. A red ochre-tinted batter, smooth and pliable.

There was a story you told yourself about what happened on the day of your great-grandmother's death.

Ritual mourners and revelers danced, beat their chests, flung themselves around the open courtyard of her house, around her corpse sheathed in parrot-green silk, around the makeshift wooden throne on which she was seated. Your emotions crashed against the sobs of the oppari, the pounding array of the marana gaana drums, the currents of flower petals, the liquor and ganja-soaked haze of her great-grandchildren, of her grandchildren, of her children from an assortment of men—for she had pledged fealty only to a single husband, but not to a single bed.

A too-quick moment, a wedge of carelessness. Perhaps that was when your great-grandmother slid under your skin, slid under the corded ropes of your musculature. Perhaps that was when she pulled apart the jewel-red slab of your liver and relaxed into its slick warmth.

Perhaps it was because you did not arrange your
face into an expression of grief, choosing to sip from a
thimbleful of boredom instead.

Perhaps that was the story you told yourself.

A boy, loved from afar.

*Batter ladled into muslin-lined pans. A swell of newly-steamed
idlis. Blush-colored, fragrant.*

The days smeared into her memories. You were
an insignificant great-grandchild, certainly not her
favorite, not her least-favorite either. Ordinary, routine,
expendable. There were aspirations that you had once
claimed as your own, once held within cupped palms—
the cool logic of statistical data, helices of numbers,
spiraled equations.

After she moved into the chalk blue antechamber of
your portal vein, taking up space as only she knew how
to do, as only she ever did, her voice insistently scraped
against your skull. Your aspirations dulled into fog.

Night after night, you fell asleep into her dreams, into
her cravings, the smoke from her suruttu cigars wisping
through your esophagus. On waking, the sweat-slicked
faces of her lovers scattered into pearlescent clouds.

I invited someone, she rasped one morning. *For you.*

In your left ear, a perilymph sea. Gleaming waves
eddied against your ear's walls, rushing into the loops and
spirals of its bony labyrinth, forming endolymphatic tidal
pools in its wake. This was where you felt his presence
first—the tiny splashes of his footsteps echoing in the
passageways of your cochlea.

Many years ago, after receiving a series of kindnesses
from an upperclassman at school, you tripped, bent,
fell face-forwards into your feelings for him. *Kathir,*
you mouthed his name, felt its sharp cadences rip your
throat. *Kathir,* you'd sigh yourself to sleep. You kept these
feelings hidden, nestled carefully under the folds of your

indifference. Kathir with the astonishing eyelashes and the astonishing calves, who would have never looked at someone such as yourself—a diminutive, funnel-chested boy.

And yet, there he was. He raked his fingers across the sponge of your vestibular duct as he walked through its corridors. Your ears bled, scabbed over, bled again.

I didn't know you were dead. I'm sorry, you whispered one day. *I loved you, I love*—your voice trailed off.

Kathir seemed to pause.

I know, he said simply, his low murmur filming over your eyelids, the skin on the back of your neck. *I'm sorry too.*

And at night, he was gone. Your ears rang with tinnitus in his absence; a familiar, comforting song.

ENEMY COUSINS.

Blistering idlis fed into a sevainaazhi. Long strands of rice noodles disentangle themselves from the sieve.

Vaguely-formed cousins teemed around the knobs of your femurs, like ravenous aphids. They skidded down each shaft; tearing through the petal-soft musculature that clung to the uneven ridges of your linea aspera. Your thighs itched for an entire week.

My cousins are all alive, you finally said, in exhaustion. *Who are you people?*

A warning swell rippled against your abdomen. *They're my cousins,* your great-grandmother answered. *It is not your concern.*

A momentary calm washed through you. The word *concern* bounced around and clattered to a standstill within the hollow citadel of your body. When your great-grandmother had been alive, you wondered if she had known your father, your father's father, your name. As its intervertebral discs clicked softly into place, your spinal column began to shift and turn in anger. You finally sat upright with the shining beacon of purpose, of what needed to be done.

BOUNTY.

Jaggery. Black peppercorns. Desiccated Coconut. Woven rice noodles in pastel hues, spun into idiyappams.

The voices of your great-grandmother and her cousins keened through the pores of your forehead, your cheeks, wrists. A frenetic pulsing hammered across your limbs, threatening to split your skin open into two papery halves.

Holding your jaw in a firm edge, you toiled in the kitchen as you readied the dishes, melting misshapen cones of jaggery into a deep, golden liquid—a slurry poured over steaming idiyappams, topped with glistening raisins and cashews. The first batch was always sweet.

For the second batch—always savory—you sautéed black peppercorns, birds-eye chili halves, and wisps of desiccated coconut in cold-pressed sesame oil, poured over another steaming pile of idiyappams.

And now, the meal.

Untying the lacy knots of the rice noodles, you consumed each strand with methodical precision—your fingertips sticky with a hot, pungent sweetness. Voices softened into silence as you sated your hunger, your great-grandmother's, your familial lesions in need of tending.

Your stomach bloats. You felt no sensation, heard no sound, except the food sliding into your throat, your hands scraping against the plate.

DUPPY

BENDI BARRETT

DUPPY, noun. A haunting spirit, ghost, or other malevolent spirit out of West Indian folklore.

BANISHMENT

To get him out is to repudiate the idea of him; you have to want him gone. The specter lurking in your heart, hand hovering over your groin, until you can almost feel the heat of him in your marrow. You can be rid of him, if you want it.

First open your pilfered hotel bible to Psalm 23 and search for frankincense and myrrh. Call your grandmother and ask her how to banish a duppy.

INVITATION

To invite him in is to revere the essence of him, a lover who is smoke and shadow. If you desire, he can slip inside you, as deft as a lover's lie and ominous as the tax man. You can be adjoined to him, if you want it.

First steep black tea in lemon juice until you achieve the bitterness of your father, and form no right angles with your arms. Sleep naked under soft sheets and feel the way they tempt your soft hairs.

These rituals will not make him abandon you, but they will prove your resilience; he is craven, and you are food.

Place a scotch bonnet pepper under your tongue for as long as you can bear it. Wear white and jump over a fire three times. Cut your language. Bare your teeth. Become the blade he fears to wield.

Never walk backward into a room and throw salt into the corners of a ruined house. You are a ruined house. Your father crossed the ocean and planted you in this rocky soil. A nation in collapse and you its rotted get. Yet poisoned fruit is sweet to the poisoner.

Ask yourself if you desire freedom over adoration. For he adores you, the king of shadow—he wishes to stroke the short, coarse hairs between your thighs and taste the musk of you. To be truly free is to be alone.

These rituals will not make him love you, but devotion and craving are his food.

Season yourself with a dab of scotch bonnet pepper oil on your neck like perfume. Turn off the lights and expose yourself to the shadows after nightfall, see how they part for him. Part for him. He is the crown and you the veil.

Eat only bitter foods, avoid the sweet, and let your fingers make you pliant before you move on to grosser means. Become a ruined house. Your mother crossed the sea and swaddled you in a cracked and starry flag. A nation of promise and each of them broken. Yet no fruit is disappointing to the hungry.

Ask yourself if you can bear to be the object of lust. For he lusts after you, the lord of whispers—he wishes to lick the sweat from between your shoulder blades and catalog the sounds you make when you erupt. To be truly adored is to be consumed.

Pour fresh water into a
white enamel basin and
leave it out in the sun
for a day. Sprinkle the
water over everything you
love. Breathe in the scent
of it. Like fresh air and
folk magic. Close your
eyes. Imagine the sun.
Imagine the light, burning
your dark skin darker,
so dark you disappear in
overexposed photos with
your paler lovers.

Give yourself over to
the Lord of your mother.
Submit to wide-eyed terror
and ecstasy. Recall the
time you took mushrooms
and fell wailing in the sight
of a God whose burning
eye pierced you through
cloud, through tree cover,
and could see your naked
body writhing beneath
your clothes. Deliverance
is first abandonment, then
discovery; those who are
not lost will not be found.

Cut the tarot deck; draw
the Eight of Swords and
draw the Eight of Swords
again. Turn the deck in
your hand and reveal that
every card is the Eight of
Swords. Breathe in the
scent of it. Like brimstone
and obeah. Close your
eyes. Imagine the garden.
Imagine the snake,
binding your hands and
legs, slipping sliced fruit
between your lips.

Give yourself over to
the skepticism of your
father. Submit to the terror
and wide-eyed ecstasy
of intimacy. Recall the
time you met a priest in a
rectory, how he locked the
door from the inside with
a key, recall the enormous
crucifix over his door and
the leather harness lying
on his bed. Recall the wine
he served and how it was
so sweet in your mouth.
The soul is the thing we
name our subjectivity;
those who see others are
God.

When you are ready,
place a robe over your
bare shoulders and marvel
at its softness. Step into a
pair of boxer briefs that
hug you just so and take
solace in the divinity of
the fit. Make dumplings
in the kitchen and knead
the dough with your
fingers and palm until
it forms the shapes that
your grandmother's
grandmother knew. He is
banished in the present:
the moments of focus and
clarity when the mind is
alive and wanton. Listen
for the throb of your own
heartbeat. The pulse. The
pulse. Roll the flour, press
hard, turn him away.

When you are ready,
lift the shirt from your
chest and fold it neatly.
Slip your briefs down your
hips and tuck its corners
into itself. Step into the
too-hot waters of the bath
and exhale what ails you;
breathe in what makes you
whole. He is found in the
interstitials: the moments
of quiet when the body is
alive and wanton. Listen
in the buzzing silence for
the knock. The knock. The
knock. Turn your head,
touch your breast, let him
in.

THE HERON-GIRL

MARI NESS

FALL, FOR ANGELA, meant waiting by the lake.
Sometimes in October, when the heavy heat and
the rains still lingered, trapping her in the house,
forcing her to watch the lake through the windows.
Sometimes in November, when it could get unexpectedly
cold, leaving her shivering on the boat dock. Sometimes as
late as December, which still had its warm days, when she
could sit by the lake and pretend to be busy, even as she
waited.

Sometimes for nothing.

Sometimes for only a feather.

Sometimes—

*don't get your hopes up please come please come please don't get
your hopes up please come please come don't get your hopes up please
come I can't lose this I can't*

—for a great blue heron to touch down on the waters,
and *shimmer.*

It would be pure chaos right after that. The girl
never seemed to know how to swim, and always seemed
unexpectedly heavy with earth and water until she even
more unexpectedly became light as air again, throwing

Angela completely off balance. Sometimes, too, she was bleeding, which terrified Angela—what if the nearby gators could smell the blood? This lake was a favorite hideout of theirs: wide and shallow, with few humans or boats. Sometimes she would spot them swimming nearby as she waited, her heart leaping into her throat. *Not now not now not now*—

And then the chaos of pulling the girl up to the boat dock, and trying to get her up into the house before anyone saw Angela half helping, half dragging, a naked girl into the house. A naked girl shedding feathers.

And then the touch of wind and air on lips and skin.

I can't lose this I can't—

†

AND YET HERE she was, watching the churning waters of the ocean instead of the calm waters of the lake.

Angela could not have said why, exactly, she turned to the east after leaving the airport instead of the west. It was not exactly a longing for the ocean—she had seen a different part of it just a week before, and the heron-girl never objected to a drive to the beach. It was not the knowledge that she had plenty of time—even November was sliding by, and the heron-girl would not come after December, if she came at all. It was not that she had anything to do here, other than watch the waves. Or a lack of desire—even now, after all these years, the mere thought of the heron-girl was enough to make Angela catch her breath, and shiver.

And yet.

I can't—

It was not *quite* the same desire.

—give this up I can't I can't

Impossible not to recognize that while Angela had changed, the heron-girl hadn't. Impossible not to remember the stranger who had assumed the heron-girl was her daughter; impossible to forget the looks they had gotten when Angela had kissed her last year in the nature reserve. Impossible to forget the questioning glances from the few friends who had met them both, friends who just a few years ago had joked about miraculous moisturizers, and now—

It had been a mistake to introduce the heron-girl to those friends.

Impossible not to recognize the pain she felt whenever she glimpsed a great blue heron.

Impossible not to realize just how little time she spent with the heron-girl each year. Three months, maybe four. Glorious months, always.

Impossible to ignore that even now, after all of these years, she didn't know the heron-girl's *name*. The heron-girl never spoke, and although she knew how to read—Angela often caught her curled up with a book or tablet, so intent that she did not seem to hear Angela's voice—she did not, or would not, write. *Heron-girl*, Angela called her, or *Sky* when she needed to mention her to others, but neither felt right.

Impossible to forget that she knew nothing of the heron-girl's *other* life, her life of spring and summer. Did she remain a heron? Or did she change into a girl again on a different lake? Did she have another lover? Angela was not jealous—she *wasn't*—but it was so frustrating not to know. Not when she spent the winter months telling the heron-girl everything—*everything*—as they held each other on the couch, or danced on the porch and the grass that ran down to the lake. Not when Angela had never taken another lover, not because of any promises, but because she *knew* that no one else could compare to the heron-girl.

Impossible to forget that the heron-girl was not, and never had been, a *girl*.

And yet.

Angela knew what her life was without the heron-girl. Knew that life was why she left every spring, telling the neighbours that she simply could not take the summer heat. It was true in a way—she was always ill after the heron-girl left, always in pain—and yet not why she fled the house. Not why she buried herself in work during the summer months, churning out illustration after illustration, trying to capture just a sliver of what she felt when the heron-girl placed a soft finger on her skin.

Knew that none of her illustrations were as good as the ones she created when the heron-girl was in the same house, watching the sky.

Knew that time did not stop for her, even if it did for the heron-girl.

She listened to the ocean, trying to forget the sound of wings, even as seagulls cried above her.

†

But she did return to the lake, did drag the heron-girl from the water, did spend the next few cold weeks locked in the girl's embrace.

Did follow her back down to the boat dock as the days lengthened, and the heat returned.

"Will you return?"

The heron-girl did not answer, even with a kiss.

And yet as Angela walked back to the house, she clutched a long grey-blue feather in her hand, so tightly she did not even feel it work its way into her skin.

Horoscopes from the Trappist-1 e Gazette

Tessa Fisher

Horoscopes are calculated with the assumption of birth or initialization on TRAPPIST-1 e. For those born or activated on c, f, or g, please see the Outer Stations supplement.

Today's Birthday: 7th orbit 3 104 AL (October 10th, 2382).
   Good fortune will come to you in the next orbit! The heavens look favorably upon your future ventures, and you will have the opportunity to achieve your most cherished dreams. While it may seem like uncertainty is everywhere, from sightings of Coleoptoid scout ships to unexpected solar flares, know that your success is all but guaranteed. Just make sure not to let it all go to your head!

Vehiculum, the Re-Entry Vehicle (Hours 0-12)
   As TRAPPIST-1 h leaves your sign, expect a change of fortune, this time for the better. Financial stability will improve as long as you keep a clear and cool head, though h's lingering influence cautions against nanofoundry investments. Be open to new possibilities from places that might surprise you. A Salix in particular may be the bearer of good news, so be on the lookout.

FALX, THE SCYTHE (HOURS 12-24)

This is a time of abundance! Expect a flourishing in your creative abilities whether it's designing new AI cores or arranging the gossenberry plants in your garden. If you'd thought about taking up a new hobby, now is the ideal time. It is said that great art emerges from periods of crisis and upheaval. Rather than just fret about possible approaching war fleets, let your muse sing to you, and see what you can contribute. You may find yourself going down in the (surviving) history archives!

SERPENSCAELO, THE SKY-SNAKE (HOURS 24-48)

TRAPPIST-1 and g are currently warring for dominance in your sign, so prepare yourself for more strife than a Coleoptoid at a human diplomatic banquet; be sure to refrain from following their example and metaphorically eating the human envoys as an appetizer! You will receive conflicting commands and requests from the higher-ups—trust your intuition to make the right choice of which to heed. Relationships may suffer, so be sure to up your communications with any and all partner(s). It's going to be a rough ride, but kindness to yourself and others will see you through.

GLORIA, THE BUTTERFLY (HOURS 48-60)

Fortunately, the conjunction of b and c will shield you from the turmoil occurring in neighboring Serpenscaelo. This power duo will lend you a boost in confidence, be sure not to waste it! Ask for that promotion you deserve. Ask that gorgeous synthetic across the hall on a date. Get that phenotype modification that you've been longing for. A strong sense of self will get you noticed by all the right people, and you'll find friends and family never fail to be supportive of your decisions. This orbit, the only limit you have is yourself.

SALTATOR, THE DANCER (HOURS 60-72)

You've been running yourself ragged as of late, but with d entering your sign, it's time for you to take a well-deserved rest. Sleep late if you have to, and feel free to stop and smell the pseudoroses. Avoid any intra-system travel—it will just stress you out more than it's worth. It's fine to worry about a Coleoptoid invasion, but don't worry too much. Just remember, no matter how chaotic life may seem, you've got things under control.

FALSORYX, THE FANTALOPE (HOURS 72-84)

Just as the fantalopes follow their endless, circum-planetary migration along the Dawn Rim, you, too, shall feel a deep sense of wanderlust. Expect invitations from old friends, and plenty of excuses to travel, physically or mentally. A change in surroundings, no matter how temporary, will be of great benefit to you, especially given the stress we've all been living under lately. Be ready to broaden your horizons. A Tenebra would make an excellent traveling companion.

SALIX, THE WILLOW (HOURS 84-96)

The bottom isn't going to fall out this orbit, but it will still feel like it has. Trouble may come in the form of a sputtering fusion reactor, a neglected lover, or a rampant AI. This orbit is a test of your character under pressure. Avoid any impulse shopping sprees or phenotype alterations—you'll thank yourself later. On the bright side, look for things to improve in the coming orbits, as TRAPPIST-1 always shines most brightly after the solar storm, Coleoptoid invasion or no Coleoptoid invasion.

ASTRONAUT, THE SPACER (HOURS 96-108)

Family is key this orbit as challenges approach. Whether it's your parents, your children, your partners, or your genetic derivatives, all hands will need to be on deck. It's not all bad news, as this will be an excellent opportunity to strengthen your bonds. Remember where you came from, and what that means to you, and you'll make it through unscathed.

HELICIS, THE DNA MOLECULE (HOURS 108-120)

When did things get so complicated? Relationships, job responsibilities, and personal commitments threaten to overwhelm you, and a personal assistant AI can only help so much. There has never been a better time to simplify, and doing so will be heartily rewarded. Avoid any political entanglements, whether intra-system or out-system: if you want a seat at the table, wait until next month. Right now, you'll just be served as the main course.

CLAMATOR, THE FOREST HOWLER (HOURS 120-132)

This is your orbit for love! If you're looking to start a new relationship, or deepen your current one(s), be open to inspiration from surprising sources. However, as hard as it might be for Clamators, be sure to take things slowly—this one is definitely for keeps. Your heart or other primary circulatory pump will let you know when you've found the right one. You have particularly good chances with Astronauts since they'll need a helping hand this orbit.

Terebra, the Drill (Hours 132-144)

As f rises in your sign this orbit, you'll relish being in good health. Athletic accomplishments are easy for you, so plan accordingly. You may be tempted to overdo it, however, and must fight against this tendency—you can only push yourself so hard before it starts to wear you down. Know your limits, and you should expect a long and prosperous life. Unless you're the one the Coleoptoids end up eating for dinner, of course.

CBROTHER ONE-WING

S. M. HALLOW

*A*T NIGHT, WHEN he and his swan brothers lift into the air like six white ghosts, he opens his beak against the sky and pretends to eat the stars. When they skitter into landing on the moonlit lake, he sinks his elegant neck beneath the water and thinks, *I am swallowing the moon whole.* He cannot say whether his five brothers ever take to the air with liberated joy, or if they ever feel embraced by a splash, but he does. Every time.

He does not yet know that one day he will awake to a single useless wing, and that all the world will know him for it and call him Brother One Wing. Beside him will lay a lover he has yet to meet, a huntsman with broad shoulders and a beard like lamb's wool. The freedom he knows now isn't a freedom that will last. In a story like this, it can't.

†

ONE DAY, HIS sister will be a queen.

Today, she's a girl who lives in a hovel in the woods.

She tosses kernels of corn and unshelled peas into the grass for her brothers then leaves them to squabble over who will win the biggest share. Threading thorns through the eye of a needle, she continues the wretched work of breaking a curse. Six shirts for six swan brothers in six silent years, or they'll never be human again.

Of his brothers, he's the one who tugs at the ragged hem of her dress for her attention. As she stains his feathers with her blistered hand, he thinks about biting her and making her scream. One sound out of her and they'll be swans forever.

But he can't do that to his brothers, or to her. Look at them: love traps them both in silence. He wishes he had a voice to tell her what he wants.

His isn't the wish the story cares about.

†

LONG BEFORE SHE sees the king, she hears his dogs howling on the hunt. Knee-deep in filth and magic, he'll see her as either a witch or a princess—and though neither is wholly untrue, she doesn't have time for the consequences of her nature. There's work to do.

So she takes her work high into the nearest tree, and perches atop a branch to keep sewing. The story is already written. Before she even meets the king, she's his wife. Before she even sees him, she has his children. Before she even makes her choice, she's on the pyre, accused of murder.

Some stories have endings before they begin.

†

AS FOR THE huntsman, he's always had choices, but this takes years to understand. As he aims his arrow at her heart, he sees the wicked queen's stepdaughter for the first time, younger and more beautiful—and he knows this story is hers.

The huntsman realizes he can walk away at any moment, and this is the moment he chooses.

He lets the poor girl go. Let whatever happens happen. He doesn't stay to see how this story ends.

†

ONE MORNING, AWAKING in bed together, Brother One Wing smooths his fingers through the thick curls of the huntsman's hair. "What did you dream of?" he asks.

"I can't speak of it," the huntsman says.

Despite all the years they've spent together, the huntsman never confesses to the horrible things he's done. Brother One Wing can't imagine what it's like to bury one's past as if it were dead. His own past still lives, still has a heartbeat, in the remaining wing that never regressed to armhood.

†

WHEN HE FLIES toward her pyre, he knows that this is the end of him. Last in the swooping line, he watches each of his brothers receive shirts and become men again. That's all they want: to become men again, even if she burns. The shirt falls over him, stinging with its nettles, and sinks deeper than bone, and the first words he speaks are in her defense.

†

SOME WINTER, WALKING with her through the village square, Brother One Wing offers his sister his wing to hold. She refuses. She never believes him when he promises he is happy.

At the tailor, she observes the work required to create a coat that can accommodate a wing. Children gather around him and hound him for stories and, raising his wing high and spreading his feathers, he promises to regale them another time. The baker gives him a loaf of daily bread, which he cradles with his wing. With his true hand, he holds the box given to him by the cobbler, containing a surprise for his huntsman.

Through all this, the queen sees her shortcomings, and a promise she could not keep.

At the edge of the village, beyond all roads, they discover a pond. Even in winter, with a thin veil of ice masking the surface, a pair of swans sit together. The queen lowers her head and keeps walking. Brother One Wing pauses to watch the swans in their act of living.

"I've realized something," Brother One Wing says. "The best years of my life were the worst years of yours."

He smiles, and takes his sister's hand to place it on his wing.

"Our brothers forget," he says, "but I never wanted to."

†

THE DAY BROTHER One Wing and the huntsman meet, they have no idea what they will become. Seeing that white wing, the huntsman asks: "What was it like, then?"

Brother One Wing always wants to tell the story, but no one ever asks. Like his sister, most people presume his shame, rather than his joy.

"It taught me humility," Brother One Wing says. "It taught me there is more to this world worth caring about than money and glory. I never thought the plants that grow in the lakebed could taste more delicious than a feast served to me on golden platters, but they did. And to move through the water with the ease of belonging, to feel it roll off your back… I didn't know I could be that happy."

The next day, the huntsman decides: no more geese, no more ducks. No bird will know his arrow again.

†

In the quiet defenselessness that borders sleep, the huntsman drags his calloused fingertips down the cascade of white feathers and asks: "Do you miss it? Would you go back?"

Brother One Wing nestles his head closer into the crook of the huntsman's shoulder and drapes wing over chest. "How can I go back," he asks, "if I can't leave it behind?"

That isn't the answer to the question he was asked, but it is the closest answer he can give. The huntsman cards his fingers through the feathers, deepening his touch until he feels skin and the curve of bone. When they kiss, Brother One Wing feels the huntsman everywhere, like air, like wind.

An Island in His Splendor

Christopher Caldwell

THE SUMMER AFTER Octavio Paz died, Eric stood on the rocks below Point Dume and tried to cast his heart into the sea. Lips swollen from crying, eyes puffy from sleeplessness, dizzy from grief, he invoked the compact he made as a child with a creature from the depths. His voice croaked. "Flounder, flounder in the sea, come up from the depths for me! Though you may not care for my request, I've come to ask it nonetheless."

The day was still and hot, but a salt wind whipped over the waves and the tide surged to crest around the rocks. A dark shape rose from the water, bigger even than the last time. An enormous sand dab, the size of a Buick Roadmaster, turned yellowed eyes on the same side of its head towards Eric. The fish's voice grated like a knife on slate. "It hasn't quite been a year. I would think the last time would give you pause."

Eric rolled up the sleeve of his shirt. Iridescent scales shone blue and peacock green against the sand brown of his left arm. He ran his fingers through his naps, winced as they caught a tangle in his kitchen. "I have the power to transfix men's gaze. I have the power to ensnare hearts.

What's the use if I have to feel like this?"

The sideways mouth opened and closed. "Young love?"

Tears stung Eric's eyes. "When Andy moved back home last year, everything was gray. Then in April, I met Donte. Not at the Catch, not at the Library, not in heels and satin, but as me. Just *me*. Outside the Abbey drinking coffee." Eric hiccupped. "His favorite poet had just died, and there was whiskey on his breath and stubble on his cheek, and he dragged me back into color."

"What are you asking me?"

Eric pulled at his shirt. "I don't want to feel like this anymore! I don't want to care about things! Take the part of me that hurts! I don't want it."

The fish's voice was low and mournful. "You did me a kindness when it was in your power. I will do you a hard kindness now. You do not want to close off your heart."

"Where were you when my city burned?"

The fish said, "I could make you forget."

Eric thought of a night in the canyons, the chaparral rising towards the stars like smoke in the blackness. Kisses along the line of his chin. Poems in Spanish. The word *pájaro* whispered so it fluttered at his throat, and then a murmuration of starlings breaking into clouds and swirls overhead as if they were summoned. He closed his eyes. "I don't want to forget."

"You can bring him back. You can make him stay."

Eric knew both of these things were true. And there was a moment after Donte said he hoped they would remain friends when an ugly, vicious part of Eric wanted Donte to wriggle like a fish on the end of a hook. He shook his head. "I don't want him as a husk. I don't want him to stay because he has to. I want him to want to."

The fish said, "He wouldn't know the difference."

"I would know! You said you would help me when I called. Well, I called. Help me not feel like this!"

The fish rasped, "You know the costs."

"I don't care if I sprout gills." Eric sank to his knees. "Just make this stop."

The fish said, "Compassion is a rare thing. I will not take that from you. But I will teach you a thing."

The fish said a word that hung in the air and rumbled against the rocky promontory. Eric felt a familiar pain in his right arm; glittering scales sprouted to match his left. The ocean roared. A wave crested and grew narrow as it approached the shore, crashing over Eric and grasping him in an icy hand. He exhaled in surprise. Water constricted around his waist, pressing in on him like a corset. The cold was nearly unbearable until he felt softness against his skin. Instead of wetness, there was silk. The cruel wave had transformed into couture. His bodice was covered in seed pearls and tiny sequins with the same iridescence as the scales on his arms. The gown flowed from his hips into a skirt the green of sea glass. He took a breath, feeling comforted by its snugness. Where there had been confusion, heartache, and the raw resentment of loneliness, Eric felt cool, calm, and confident.

The fish spoke the word again. It shimmered in the air and bloomed as a sigil in Eric's mind; he knew he could call on that strange, cold wave again.

The fish sunk beneath the surface. Eric heard its voice on the wind. "Clothe yourself in the ocean when the world is too much to bear. Submerged you will remain as sharp, glittering, and cold as an icicle. When you are ready to surface, you shall return intact, but renewed and radiant as the dawn."

Eric turned his back to the ocean. The sun sank low on the horizon, burnishing his gown bronze and gold. City lights floated across the water as evening came on; curtain call at the Library was at eight.

Choosing

Susan Taitel

THE SILENT GIRL concerns you. You're told she materialized from the sea, naked and speechless. She follows your betrothed like a besotted puppy and dances with a grace that makes your chest constrict. Nevertheless, her agony is evident in every step. She has no name and apparently no past. Yet she's a mystery that troubles no one but you.

You try to show her kindness—she seems to need it— but you are overwhelmed by the preparations for your wedding. You're only fifteen; you do not wish to marry. You campaigned tirelessly to be sent to the temple. It was the first time, the only time, you stood up to your parents and demanded to be heard. And remarkably, after months of arguing, you were.

You had just begun your education, just glimpsed what your life could be, when you found a man lying facedown on the beach. He was half-drowned, shivering and delirious. You couldn't know that when you brought him inside and sat him in front of the fire to stop his teeth from chattering you had sealed your fate. But when a prince declares you the only woman in the world for him, and your parents, recognizing a profitable alliance, give their enthusiastic consent, what choice do you have?

Many choices actually, none of which matter. How many gowns for your trousseau? Which strangers from your fiancé's court will be your ladies-in-waiting? A diadem or a floral wreath for the wedding? Every choice made leads to a dozen more. You begin choosing at random.

This frees you to focus on the silent girl. You have yet to find a puzzle you could not solve if given enough time. You request that she be added to your retinue. You attempt to find ways to communicate that do not require a voice but she is reticent. You show her maps, hoping she will identify her homeland. Despite your best efforts, you learn nothing new. The only thing you are certain of is that she is in love with your husband-to-be. You come to realize that your presence is compounding her pain. You are nothing but a reminder that the one she loves has chosen another. You yearn to tell her that you are equally unhappy with his choice, but the duchess tasked with molding you into an appropriate bride for a prince is seldom out of earshot.

On the day you are to be wed, your mother tells you what to expect from the wedding night. You listen with growing distaste. Once, at the temple, when it was your morning to call the scholars to breakfast, you found two of the girls entwined in the same bed. Theoretically, this option is slightly more appealing than the alternative, but for you, your body is little more than a container for your mind. In your studies of biology, you researched the reproductive habits of animals; you are aware of the mechanics. That it would one day apply to you was unfathomable.

You are so rattled by what is to come, you barely notice the ceremony or the following soiree. You don't remember reciting the vows. Yet you must have; you are irrevocably

married. You come back to yourself when the silent girl
performs a solo ballet. A dance of impossible beauty and
sorrow that causes you to weep into your veil.

After the party, you board the wedding ship. You're
led to the bridal suite where you change behind a screen,
climb into the bed, and squeeze your eyes shut. Your
husband, it seems, over-celebrated your union. He passes
out beside you. One night's reprieve.

You are woken by ragged breathing in the dark. The
silent girl stands over you, a knife clutched in her hand.
She's trembling, staring at your husband. You wait,
frozen, for her to strike. You don't know which of you is
her intended victim. A scream will summon help. You
remain silent.

She exhales, drops the knife, and leaves.

You untangle yourself from the sheets and the stifling
warmth of the stranger you married. You pick the knife
from the carpet and follow the girl to the deck. She stands
at the rail, silhouetted by moonlight. She sways and goes
limp. You catch her. She stares up at you, panic in her
eyes. You signal reassurances and offer her the knife. She
steps back, looking to you and then to the water.

A song swells up from the sea. Voices singing of
freedom and fate. She closes her eyes. The distress slowly
fades from her face; she opens her eyes, her decision made.
She takes two running steps and dives over the side. You
reach for her, but she's gone. No splash, only froth. You
stare at the water, tears on your cheeks.

The knife rests in your hands. Your husband still sleeps.
You may come to love him or at least grow fond of him.
You have a choice to make.

The knife severs the rope, sending your lifeboat
bobbing away from the larger ship. The prince will wake
to find both his pet and his bride missing. One drowned,
one fled. It hardly matters which.

The sisters at the temple will hide you for a short time.

Eventually, someone, your parents or the prince, will think to look for you there. You must make good use of your time. You dip your hand into the water, letting it skim along the surface. An unspoken farewell to the silent girl. You smile as the ship disappears from view. You have so many choices ahead of you.

THE RABBI

ESTHER ALTER

I HAD FORGOTTEN which dating app I met Leah on, but it was either the dating app where I masqueraded as a crossdressing man interested in women or the dating app where I masqueraded as a confident lesbian. We got to talking about being Jewish around the time we started teasing each other with the promise of nudes and rope. I'd thought of myself as the sort of Jew who went to services to appease my parents, on Rosh Hashanah, and when I felt guilty. I told Leah that I'd been taught that God had made my body exactly as it was, and that it was a sin to modify it. I didn't really believe it but I'd never been able to shake it off. Leah messaged: *The Rabbi will make you into a woman.*

I believed her. I didn't even text back, *What are you talking about?*

Leah sent me a sloppily-composed photo of three women, nude, kneeling on the floor with their arms behind them, leather straps criss crossing up to a tefillin box on their deferential heads. In the right corner of the image was a blurred presence that seemed to bend all of the pixels into it. Leah said that she was the kneeling woman in the center. I told Leah I was feeling too shy to send a photo of myself.

I waited for Leah to text back before giving up, jerking off, and going to bed. Then, the following evening, I received a message. *This is the Rabbi. Leah has told me all about you. Listen: You are a part of God's creation, destroyed once in the Flood, and now ours to repair. In your imperfection you yet hold the spark of the divine. I can reveal God's sacred truth within you, if you serve me.*

What do you want from me? I texted back.

Reveal yourself to me, the Rabbi replied. *Show me your face, and your chest, and your tits, as an offering to me.*

I logged off and took a cold shower and went to bed early. I woke up an hour later.

Is this a cult? I texted.

The Rabbi replied: *I'll only ever take what you give willingly.*

I lurched to the bathroom, took off my shirt in front of the sink mirror and sent the Rabbi a picture of my ashkenazily hairy chest.

Yes, Yes! the Rabbi texted back. *Beautiful as the Moon! Obedient as Ruth!*

I need to be someone else, I insisted.

If that is all you need, God will provide, said the Rabbi.

I need you to make me someone else, I said.

This, said the Rabbi, *is another matter entirely. For this, you must give yourself to me. I need your body. I need your eyes. I need your hair, and your ass, and your dreams.*

Her congregation was only a few towns over, and the virus was still mostly just bad news, so I signed a new lease for a one-bedroom with a rat problem. The synagogue was an old Victorian a ten-minute walk away, right next to a bodega.

By the time I finished moving in, the streets were empty, and the bodega shelves were bare except mustard for some reason. I took two bottles of mustard and ran home. I might've forgotten to pay.

The Rabbi invited me to a video chat and I joined it. Her webcam was off, but I heard her voice, clear as the blast of a shofar. "Are you staying safe?" she asked.

"As I am able. You?"

The Rabbi said, "No virus may harm me."

"Bullshit," I said.

"I tested negative."

"Your women?" I asked. "Leah?"

"Also tested negative. They haven't left my house. They begged me to chain them to the wall," the Rabbi said.

"Take me," I said. "Chain me."

"Do you know if you're infected?"

"No," I admitted.

I heard her shrug rabbinically.

"Is there any way I can serve you?" I asked.

"Like this?" the Rabbi said. "No."

"Let me at least see you," I said.

"I won't allow that," she replied swiftly. "You may not see my face until you are ready to serve me."

"Let me see something, anything," I begged.

Silence. And then: Behold! The sleek polished leather of a boot. The hands of the divine feminine, unlacing it. Sliding it off. An ankle revealed. A heel, an arch, and toes. All of this passed before me and then the video feed went black. All of this I saw and I knew then that I would do whatever I could to survive, for her.

Some day, the bell curve, in its cosmically perfect indifference, will abate. On that day, I will go to the house of my Rabbi. One of her women will open the door for me and beckon me in. I will affix a kippah to my head and remove my clothes. I will get on my knees, and I will be led, crawling, across the hallowed floor to her. And then, I will begin anew.

OUR DAYS OF
TEAR-STAINED GLASS

AVRA MARGARITI

OUR SHIP REMEMBERS the sea, yet the only water we know these days comes from the giant mermaid's tears. Once a mighty pirate vessel, we are now a model ship-in-a-bottle inside our abductor's grotto.

I was once known for stealing every gem from every royal crown. Now, I of a thousand rubies, am captured by the watery sapphires of the mer-giantess's eyes. I didn't know mermaid tears taste saltier than human. That the larger the body, the deeper the sorrow. I have graduated from sharpening my knives on leather belts to becoming a master desalinator. I store our drinking water into buckets, then use the remaining salt to preserve the tiny fish left in the wake of another one of her crying spells.

My work for the day finished, I drape myself over the ship's mermaid figurehead (tiny and unimportant compared to her vast beauty) and patiently wait. I want to be the first to watch her arrive, dulse-tangled hair, shipwrecks caught between her teeth, skin tinged green with the sea.

Not everyone adapts to our new routine the way I do. The old sailor—always quick to call my love for the

giantess unhealthy or remind me she doesn't give two
corals about my tiny existence—has to plug his ears each
night before going to sleep in his hammock. He hears the
song of the sea, that suicidal shanty. I once had to use
every nautical knot I know and tie him to the mast so he
wouldn't plunge overboard. The water is far away now,
undulating out past the mouth of the grotto, but he still
hears its nocturnal siren murmurs. If he jumped now, he
would become a blood-and-guts stain against the curved
glass of our bottle prison.

The captain charts desperate courses, bent over
his maps and tools, pulling at his hair until he is bald
and baby-faced. He and the old sailor used to concoct
elaborate escape plans but have long since given up, tiring
of failure. Whenever I bring his seaweed-and-minnow
stew dinner down to his cabin, he stares at me with
eyelash-less eyes. "I thought you were smarter than that
when I hired you," the captain sometimes says. "You used
to be hard as a shell, girlie, the best thief in the land."

"I was," I agree every time. But she has opened me up
like an oyster, and now my soft insides ache for the first
sight of her every day like the clockwork dawn.

The captain's parrot isn't faring any better. Once upon
a time he flew nightly to the crow's nest and serenaded
Cygnus, the swan constellation. She had almost accepted
his invitation to elope when the giantess came upon our
wave-tossed ship, snatched it from the storm, and took
us home to her collection. The parrot doesn't judge my
feelings. He knows what it's like to love impossible things.

I hang further off the edge of the figurehead to catch a
glimpse of her through the foggy, slightly distorted glass.
Why are you sad? I want to ask her. *Unburden yourself to me;
I used to know all about unburdening people of their gold and
silver, but grief is a new spoil I think I can learn to bear. Are you
sweet or salty up close? Will you let me pillow myself on your plush
shoulders? Can I have one of your shiny scales to use as a mirror?*

From now on I only want to see myself in you.

The giantess drops to the floor and the grotto shakes, our ship rattling in its bottle. I cling tighter to the figurehead and take in her form as her tears wash down the glass like a rainstorm, a watery blur. Greenbluepurple scales hug her skin, crawling up her breasts. A strong tail supports her even on land, while her hands are webbed and her teeth needle sharp. Sometimes she inserts tweezers through the bottle's throat to straighten our sails. The tweezers never come near me, although I'm not sure I would mind the pinch, as long as it came from her hands. Today she only gazes through her naked eyes and cries cries cries into the mouth of the bottle.

The old sailor curses as he mops up the saltwater that slinks its way onto the deck. His peg leg gains an easy grip onto the slippery wood floor. I descend into the ship to prepare dinner with a stupid smile on my face. My lips taste of salt.

When I return, the old sailor is still here, scowling. "Listen, I know a thing or two about loving the wrong person."

Of course he does. He had a messy love affair with the ocean once and she has been calling him to his doom ever since.

"We're not the same," I tell him.

He shakes his head morosely and wrings out his mop.

That night, after the giant mermaid has re-corked the bottle, covered it in grimy canvas, and placed us on the grotto's highest shelf, I go to sleep shivering. I dream of growing large enough to become a giantess myself. Our prison shatters, wood splinters and glass shards flying every which way and ricocheting off the stone walls.

I emerge from the rubble ready to dry her tears. To walk into her arms.

CBEYOND THE VEIL

J. KOSAKOWSKI

MANY FLOWERS GROW in the little village of Popný during Spring. It is marriage season and the air is filled with pollen. Mara collects flowers with the people who should be most important in his life: his mother, his sister, his aunts, his various cousins, and those that would be his bridesmaids.

They should be important, but they are not. They do not see him as the man he is inside and have thus arranged an early marriage for him.

A marriage to a man older than his own father.

"These flowers," his oldest aunt says, cutting all of them from their pot and placing them within Mara's basket. "For fertility. With luck, you'll give your husband his first son next year."

Mara does not weep. He may be desperately unhappy, but he is also more stubborn than their goat.

His wedding dress is ready. His shoes shine. His mother gives him a delicate lace veil to cover his face. But his family couldn't grow back the hair he had shorn close to his scalp.

If his family could not accept him as a man, then they would have to accept him as their village's ugliest, unhappiest bride.

Night is swiftly falling upon their group. Mara doesn't care. He sits upon the tall grass, bugs dancing on his legs, as those that should love him do him harm. They make two wreaths out of the flowers they had collected—one for the wedding and one for now.

Mara does not wear the wreath. He holds it in his hands grudgingly enough as he is led into the thick of the woods.

His mother sings old songs, the same she sang her youngest children to sleep with at night. Mara is the oldest and has never actually been sung to before. The oldest children are born into parenthood, many in Popný would say. Not to be cared for, but to do the caring instead. His oldest aunt joins in with her own rendition. His cousins, mere children, are so loud that they must frighten ghosts, singing about Mara's impending marriage. Mara is more than bitter that now is the only time he has been extended care.

He doesn't care, he tells himself. None of this matters.

The river Noteć is bubbling and cheerful. Silver fish swim in its blue waters.

Mara's only sister carefully places a lit candle upon a piece of wood. "Mara, your wreath," she says.

They say you can find out how fortunate your marriage will be if you throw a flower wreath into the river. Mara hands it over.

Mara's sister places the wreath around the candle. "Beautiful!" she says. "Time for you to launch it down the river."

Mara rolls his eyes. He gets a wallop across the head and a tongue-lashing from his mother. Words are just words and he is long used to being beaten. But he expects worse from his future husband.

He sighs and picks up the wooden plank, setting it down in the river and watching as it floats away.

Every bride does this. And, now, Mara.

"Many grandchildren please," says his mother, already weeping openly. "At least eight. Four big, strong boys. Four beautiful girls."

The candle wobbles on the river and then tips over. The wreath Mara's family made so carefully catches fire.

"Ah! God," his oldest aunt says, wading into the river bank. "Let it not be so!"

Mara watches and blinks.

What does it mean that the wreath caught fire?

Mara's oldest aunt lets out a cry and swoons, falling right into the river. His mother follows suit.

The temperature rises, as though the sun was breathing right on their necks. It is so hot that even Mara sways.

Slowly, Mara turns around.

A woman that Mara has never seen before joins their group. She is not one of his many family members. She is not a bridesmaid. She is dressed as a bride, resplendent in white. Her hair is braided around the crown of her head, flowers entwined with straw blonde. She holds an old sickle. When she notices him watching, she smiles.

"Noonwraith," Mara says. "Why have you come here? It is long past noon."

The noonwraith smiles sweetly. "It is midnight. This is also noon."

Mara frowns and does not argue. His cousins, his sister, and his bridesmaids are all unconscious now, their faces flushed bright red. If the noonwraith wishes to do him a kindness, then, well, he would have to take it.

"Where will you go now?" The noonwraith's skin is poreless, perfect, like that of a porcelain doll.

Mara startles badly. "I am not sure," he says. "Away."

The noonwraith tilts her head. "The man they chose as your husband. He was supposed to be mine. He was a cruel thing, even then. How many cats can you kill before a village takes notice?"

Mara waits.

"They say I killed myself," the noonwraith says. "This is not true. He killed me the night before our wedding. No one ever seemed to care about that."

Mara's heart thuds painfully in his chest. He could have been murdered too. His family would have assumed the same.

The noonwraith smiles again. "But now when he works on his farm, I take my vengeance," she tells him. "I give him heatstrokes and body aches and all sorts of wicked visions. It would not do if I also had to worry about his innocent husband."

Mara smiles for the first time he can remember. Tears drip down his cheeks.

This is the first time someone has recognized him as he is.

"Oi, no crying is allowed. I rescued you from your fate, didn't I?" She places a hand upon his cheek and he startles once again. The noonwraith is cold, colder than a grave.

"Thank you," Mara says.

The noonwraith smiles, nods, and then she is gone, leaving Mara alone with his unconscious family.

Mara pulls his oldest aunt out of the river because he is not entirely cruel, but leaves the rest of his family there on the riverbank. He looks at the remains of his wreath, now mere ash upon the river's surface, and thinks to himself, Good. Let his family think him dead.

The person they will grieve for has never existed.

Mother to None

A.Z. Louise

I AM THE last of a line, my only company the mosses that line the walls and the books I am tasked to guard. The books lie still, their pages full of songs and poems transcribed as they were spoken by long-extinct creatures, new life forms, even stones that spoke once and never again. The mosses rest between their wooden slats, insulating me from the caprices of the outside world. For many years, they too were silent, but now they whisper to me.

It began on the new moon. Though the tone grows more frantic, the words remain indecipherable, like voices speaking in the next room, where only certain syllables come through. I press my ear to the damp green mats, but the earth below the mossery is alive with fire after the most recent burn. The pops and cracks of superheated sending stones drown out the whispers. It frightens me. The earth beneath my feet is sliced through with veins of sending stone, and that someday it would have to burn, leaving empty tunnels behind. I never imagined it would be so soon.

When the world quiets enough to hear the moss, I
don't know what the words mean. The mosses have never
spoken to me before, and as I learned from the hen of the
woods, words mean different things to all the different
shapes that life takes. Still, they must be recorded.

The pages of the old, damaged books smell half of
mildew, half of sweet tobacco age. Histories of a world
eaten alive by magic. I open the book of flora with all the
care I would give to a hatching hummingbird. With an
old bottle of iron gall ink and a quill nibbled by moths, I
scratch the message into a blank page:

Soft the rain and mist
To bring a lover's kiss
Choke the neck
That fruits the spore
And thread the forest floor

Dread creeps down my spine like frost. Something is
coming. I want to huddle in the middle of my house, as far
from the mosses as possible, but I have a duty to protect
the books. If they hold no answers, there is but one place
to look.

I do not go outside often, for the trees are ancient,
their words so slow and deep that they are felt in the
bones more than heard. Trunks slant against each other
like a child's house of twigs, tied together with hungry
vines and shingled with massive lichen. Leaf litter and
other decaying things are soft under my feet, the scent
of rot mingling with the metallic stench of burning
magic that rises from below. Blue plumes of smoke and
fluttering flecks of magic make me cough and gasp for air.
They numb my lips and tongue. I press on through the
discomfort, reminding myself of my duty. Nobody else
will treasure the words of this wilderness that snatches my
breath away every chance it gets.

The ugly squash of death beneath my feet turns
to spongy softness. Moss fields stretch out ahead in a
thousand mottled shades of green, a rolling sea beneath
a sky tinged yellow with sun and spores. I lie down in the
bed of moss, warm from the sending stone fires. Here,
their song is louder than the crackle of breaking rock.

Bright the sunbeams shine
To run the anchor line
Seize the bark
Climb up the stone
And creep into the bone

Tepid rain patters against my closed eyelids. The
droplets trail down my face, a tangled web of filaments
tying me to the ground. *Thread the forest floor.* Something
shifts beneath me, the barest movement of rhizoid
tentacles. The moss is awake. I sway when I stand, dizzy
with danger. I must keep the books safe, as my mother did
before me, her mother before her.

I shamble back to the mossery, my stomach a glass
bottle on the edge of tipping over. The slow rumble of
the trees stops. The lichen only hum. Somewhere, a blue
jay makes his rusty-hinge call and falls silent. Safety flees
my home on silent wings, leaving only slats and colorful
mosses that form deadly coral snake stripes on the walls.
A hiss joins the whispers, like a thread being drawn
through the eye of a needle. The mosses pull free of their
substrates, rocking the structure to and fro. I grab as
many books as I can carry and run as the mossery lists,
shedding boards and nails, falling in on itself.

The gentle rain becomes a downpour, making lakes
out of lichen pads and pouring waterfalls into the
undergrowth. I dodge the flows, trying to protect the
books. Over my shoulder, a wave of green consumes the
mossery, the displaced air thick with the smell of earth.

Trees moan, deadwood crashes to the ground, and
saplings are crushed beneath the flow. I splash through
streams, heart too big for my ribcage.

Soaked to the bone, my nose and mouth fill with pollen
and algae washed down from the canopy. I stumble once,
twice, fall into earth churned to mud. My tomes, precious
record of a world of songs, sink into the muck. I'm elbow
deep in an instant, slogging through slime, but the delicate
goatskin parchment is ruined by the time I rescue the
books. I have no children to learn the words of the crow
or the orb weaver. I haven't seen a single human in fifteen
years at least. With the books destroyed, my work was for
nothing. The songs were my children. My lungs burn for
nothing.

I push to my knees, not knowing why. The roaming
mosses crush me flat. Rhizoids skitter over my skin, their
wet weight pushing me into the mud. The last molecule of
oxygen leaves my lungs, and for a while, I'm suspended in
time, body struggling for air that isn't there. Tendrils enter
my eardrums with two bright, searing pops, and the song
of the moss rushes in.

Dark the shadows fall
To crush and cover all
Rot the flesh
And still the mind
To leave the pain behind

Relief. My head clears as precious oxygen surges into
my lungs and words fill my veins. Every stone, every
tree, every mushroom, telling the story of rain, of river,
of flood. Lightheaded, I stagger to my feet again and
look for an escape. I scramble into an oak so ancient and
massive my arms can't fit around the trunk. The wave of
moss ripples past, and water comes behind it. Choking
steam rises from cracks in the earth, so thick that it blurs

everything except tree bark and glowing cerulean motes of magic once encapsulated by sending stones.

The world is muffled by my punctured eardrums, blood running down the sides of my face, but when the roar of water fades, silence settles in my bones, heavier than all the water in the world. If I'm free of the duty that has bound me to this place, I don't feel it. Instead, I am tied more deeply to it, the last of a dying breed the trees will forget as soon as my flesh no longer feeds them.

THE HEART IS A SPARE PART

HAILEY PIPER

I REALIZED THE town was too quiet just when I reached Gyrocore's outskirts. No rust-bucket kids running loose, no cyber-centaurs lined up outside the saloon. It seemed I was the only bot on the street, my steel feet corroded after the long stroll from the train station.

Until the Moboz Boyz burst out of town's every steam vent, all fifty of them. Seemed the whole gang was here. They'd come for a purpose, and I knew they weren't aiming to rob me; I was a scrapheap on two legs, only extraneous bit being a ten-gallon sensor-hat, to help my perspective. That perspective told me who was behind this ambush before the sun shined off his chrome.

Jagger-9000 stood behind the Moboz Boyz, top hat whirring, a platinum monocle seated at his eye, torso thrumming with extraneous gizmos out his mecha-wazoo. Those doo-dads must've cost a fortune, making him one with his riches.

We had history. Troubled history.

I'd been his bodyguard once, before I realized he was dirty. He was supposed to pay me so I could quit, but he wouldn't let me go. That data was easy to download;

seeing him every day on Gyrocore's streets was hard.
Ours became your average "This town ain't big enough
for the both of us" situation.

After clanging noggins enough, we mutually agreed
to expand the town. He funded; I built. We added the
playground, library, and dramatic theater. Town shack
grew into town hall. Part of me became fond of him, and
I didn't need my sensor-hat to see the good he could do
when he wanted.

But a scoundrel's a scoundrel, even when you love him.
Not long after Gyrocore's upgrade, I headed back east to
help my MotherBoard fend off some robo-cattle rustlers.
A slow journey there and back for a bot of my means.

While I'd been traveling, miserly subsystems prodded
Jagger-9000 to ponder all the money he could make from
taxing Gyrocore's new hardware, and there was no sheriff
bot to stop him.

The news found me on the road from Mom's: Exorbitant
library fees. Cyber-centaur parking permits. Little rust-
buckets being shaken down and thrown off the playground.
Really got my gears. Turned out my heart was leaning
toward a bad bot after all. Story of my love life.

Now, he adjusted his monocle. "You should've stayed
east."

"You should've stayed decent," I said evenly, despite
being surrounded by the Moboz Boyz. "We built this
town together, partner. Don't that mean nothing?"

Jagger-9000 got my meaning. "Check your heart's
radiator, RZ-D. Seems it's overheating again. I keep
mine cool with all my new internal tech, but the gang
here?" His hands waved his ruffians to charge. "You'll like
them—they run hot!"

I hadn't expected he'd hire help. He never paid a scrap
that he owed me, so I couldn't see him paying the Moboz
Boyz to grind me down.

But grind they did. They bolted themselves together into one giant, hundred-armed, hundred-legged mechani-pede and stomped every heel onto my scrapheap body. Blue screens of imminent demise nearly overloaded my processor. Only my sensor-hat kept me lucid.

"Don't shut him down completely," Jagger-9000 said. "Just downgrade him enough to make an example."

A bot can lose a lot of things before shutdown. The Moboz Boyz might've aimed to take my sensor-hat, seeing I didn't need it. They could really bust my radiator, leaving my heart to overheat and warp. It was a good heart, and I'd hate to need a replacement. My heart is why I ever gave Jagger-9000 a second chance. He didn't need the Moboz Boyz to bust that anyhow—in his way, he'd already broken it.

But with the Boyz busy beating me, they hadn't looted my sensor-hat yet. I could still see the decent bot I loved in Jagger-9000. Likewise, I saw the miserly bot he'd let himself become once more.

I wrenched my dented head off the ground and said, "Surprised you got your money in advance."

The mechani-pede quit stomping. "What you mean?" The Moboz Boys buzzed in unison.

"Never saw a scrap myself."

The mechani-pede turned to Jagger-9000. "You a cheat?"

Jagger-9000 rotated his monocle. "Gentlemen, I assure you my credit is pristine."

"Credit?" The mechani-pede's hundred fists clenched. "Hey, this cruelty ain't free. Pay up!"

Jagger-9000 tapped his pockets. An echo rang through his core. "I've not a scrap on me, Boyz, but we can settle up tomorrow."

The Moboz Boyz split into their fifty individual bots and surrounded Jagger-9000. "Naw, we settle up now."

They fixed their sights on his chest, where expensive gizmos thrummed. "Looks like you got plenty on you."

I didn't watch, only listened to Jagger-9000's electro-shrieking. Once the Moboz Boyz looted their pay, they ditched Gyrocore post-haste, forgetting the job they'd been brought in to do. I stood up, dirty and dented, but no worse for wear.

Couldn't say the same for Jagger-9000. The Boyz had taken everything he didn't need to function—top-hat, platinum monocle, gizmos, even his mecha-wazoo. He was a downgraded scrapheap with two legs, not an extraneous bit to him.

"That was my fortune," he said. "I'm ruined."

"Not ruined," I said. I snapped the sensor-hat off my head and handed it over. "Seems you could use a bit of perspective."

He took it, pondered its function, and then stuck it where his top hat used to sit.

I offered my hand, and he took that, too. We stood side-by-side, surveying the town we'd built. With the Moboz Boyz vanished into the horizon, the bot-folk were coming out: little rust-buckets running loose, cyber-centaurs heading for the saloon. All was right in Gyrocore once more.

I thought Jagger-9000 could see it too, maybe for the first time. At that moment, I was fixing to give my heart a reboot.

"Care for an oil change?" I asked, pointing to the saloon.

His exhaust vents blew out a sigh. "I'm sorry, RZ-D. Maybe I'd be a better bot if I had your heart."

My chest's radiator steamed. "Partner, you already got that."

CONTRIBUTORS

Esther Alter is a trans Ashkenazi Jew. Her stories, games, and programming projects can be found at subalterngames. com. Follow her on Twitter @subalterngames.

Bendi Barrett is a speculative fiction writer, game designer, and pretend-adult living in Chicago. He's published interactive novels through Choice of Games, and his novella *Empire of the Feast* is forthcoming via Neon Hemlock. He also writes gay erotic fiction as Benji Bright and runs a Patreon for the thirsty masses. He can be found at Benmakesstuff.com and on twitter as both @bendied and @benji_bright.

Jen Brown (she/her) weaves otherworldly tales about Black, queer folks righteously wielding power. An Ignyte Award nominated writer, her stories have appeared in *FIYAH Literary Magazine*, Tor.com's *Breathe FIYAH* anthology, *Baffling Magazine, Anathema: Spec From the Margins, PodCastle*, and was recently translated for Crononauta's *Matreon* publication. She tweets at @jeninthelib, & you can find more of her work at jencbrown.com.

Jacob Budenz is a queer writer, multi-disciplinary performer, educator, and witch with an MFA from University of New Orleans and a BA from Johns Hopkins. The author of *Pastel Witcheries* (Seven Kitchens Press 2018), Budenz has work in journals including *Wussy Mag, Ghost City Review, Taco Bell Quarterly*, and more as well as anthologies by Mason Jar Press, and Lycan Valley Press. At the beginning of 2020, Budenz received a Baker Innovative Projects grant to stage *Simaetha: a Dreambaby Cabaret*, at the historic Carroll Mansion in downtown Baltimore, and their collection of stories, *Tea Leaves*, is forthcoming by Amble in 2023. Follow Jake's work at jakebeearts.com or @dreambabyjake on Instagram and Twitter.

Christopher Caldwell is a queer Black American living abroad in Glasgow, Scotland. His work has appeared in *Uncanny Magazine, Strange Horizons,* and *Fiyah* among others. He is an Ignyte Awards finalist, Clarion West Alumnus, and a recipient of the Octavia E. Butler Memorial Scholarship. He is @seraph76 on twitter.

Nino Cipri is a queer and trans/nonbinary writer, editor, and educator. They are a graduate of the Clarion Writing Workshop and the University of Kansas's MFA program, and author of the award-winning debut fiction collection *Homesick* (2019) and the novellas *Finna* (2020) and *Defekt* (2021). Nino has also written plays, poetry, and radio features; performed as a dancer, actor, and puppeteer; and worked as a stagehand, bookseller, bike mechanic, and labor organizer. One time, an angry person on the internet called Nino a verbal terrorist, which was pretty funny.

Dare Segun Falowo is a writer of the Nigerian Weird. Their work draws on cinema, pulp fiction & the surreal. They are queer and neurodivergent. Their work is published in the Magazine of Fantasy & Science Fiction, the Dark Magazine and others. Their novella, "Convergence in Chorus Architecture" which appeared in the Dominion Anthology, was longlisted for the 2020 BSFA for Short Fiction. They haunt Ibadan, Nigeria where they are learning to express more of their truth in words, watercolor and spirit.

Maxwell I. Gold is an author of weird fiction and dark fantasy, writing short stories and prose that primarily center around his cosmic and profane Cyber Gods Mythos. Maxwell's work has appeared in numerous publications including *Spectral Realms, Weirdbook Magazine, The Audient Weird, Hinnon Magazine* and *Space and Time Magazine.* Maxwell studied philosophy and political science at the

University of Toledo and is a proud Columbus, Ohio native and currently is an active member of the Horror Writer's Association and the Dramatists Guild.

Tessa Fisher is a PhD candidate and possibly the world's only openly trans lesbian astrobiologist. When she's not doing science, her passions include burlesque dancing, singing in her city's LGBT women's chorus, yoga, and writing LGBT-positive science fiction and fantasy. Her work has appeared in *Vulture Bones, Fireside, Glass and Garden: Solarpunk Winters, Analog,* and is forthcoming in the anthology *Rosalind's Siblings.* She resides in Phoenix, AZ, along with her wife, and a fairly aloof bearded dragon. You can find her on Twitter @spacermase.

Jewelle Gomez is the author of four plays and seven books including the first black, lesbian vampire novel, *The Gilda Stories,* in print for more than 30 years and recently optioned by Cheryl Dunye for a TV mini-series. Find her online at jewellegomez.com and on Instagram & Twitter at @VampyreVamp.

S. M. Hallow is a comic artist and writer obsessed with fairytales. To learn more, follow Hallow on Twitter @smhallow.

Rien Gray is a queer, nonbinary author living in Ireland. Their comfort zone is dark romance and exploring trauma recovery in fiction, owing to personal experiences with C-PTSD. They have a series of F/NB romantic suspense novels with *NineStar Press,* and can be found on twitter @RienGray.

J. Kosakowski is a queer writer born and raised in New York City. While they do not enjoy long walks on the beach, they do happen to enjoy discussing all things crochet, cannibalism, and mythology. Their work has appeared in *Baffling Magazine* and *Daily Science Fiction*. They can be found at jkosakowskiwrites.wordpress.com and on Twitter @kosakowski_j.

M. L. Krishnan originally hails from the coastal shores of Tamil Nadu, India. She is a 2022-2023 MacDowell Fellow and a 2019 graduate of the Clarion West Writers' Workshop. Her work was selected for the *Best Microfiction 2022* anthology and has appeared, or is forthcoming in *The Offing, Death in the Mouth: The Best of Contemporary Horror, PodCastle, Sonora Review, Quarterly West* and elsewhere. You can find her on Twitter @emelkrishnan.

Brent Lambert is a Black, queer man who heavily believes in the transformative power of speculative fiction. He resides in San Diego but spent a lot of time moving around as a military brat. Currently, he manages the social media for *FIYAH Literary Magazine* and just had an anthology produced with Tor.com titled Breathe *FIYAH*. His novella *The Necessity of Chaos* is forthcoming from Neon Hemlock. He can be found on Twitter @brentclambert talking about the weird and the fantastic.

A.Z. Louise is a lover of birds, a writer of words, and a believer in the healing powers of peppermint tea. After leaving their job as a civil engineer, they took up poetry and fiction instead, but they still harbor a secret love of math. Links to their work can be found at azlouise.com.

Jennifer Mace is a queer Brit who roams the Pacific Northwest in search of tea and interesting plant life. A four-time Hugo-finalist podcaster for her work with Be The Serpent, she writes about strange magic and the cracks that form in society. Her anthology *Silk & Steel: A Queer Speculative Adventure Anthology,* with co-editors Django

Wexler and Janine Southard, may be ordered from any reputable purveyor of literature. Find her fiction and poetry online at englishmace.com.

Avra Margariti is a queer Social Work undergrad from Greece. She enjoys storytelling in all its forms and writes about diverse identities and experiences. Her work has appeared or is forthcoming in *Glittership, Lackington's, Fusion Fragment, Arsenika,* and other venues. You can find her on twitter @avramargariti.

Mari Ness has published poetry and fiction in *Tor.com, Clarkesworld, Lightspeed, Nightmare, Uncanny, Fireside, Strange Horizons, Diabolical Plots,* and elsewhere. Her tiny collection of tiny fairy tales, *Dancing in Silver Lands,* is available from Neon Hemlock; her poetry novella, *Through Immortal Shadows Singing,* is available from Papaveria Press, and her essay collection, *Resistance and Transformation: On Fairy Tales,* from Aqueduct Press. She lives in central Florida, where she likes to watch blue herons fly over the lakes.

Hailey Piper is the Bram Stoker Award-winning author of *Queen of Teeth, Unfortunate Elements of My Anatomy,* and *The Worm and His Kings.* Her short fiction appears in *Pseudopod, Cast of Wonders, Vastarien, Daily Science Fiction,* and elsewhere. She's an active member of the HWA, and she lives with her wife in Maryland, where the robots love Old Bay. Find her at haileypiper.com or on Twitter via @HaileyPiperSays.

Brian Rappatta's short fiction has appeared in venues such as *Analog,* Writers of the Future, *Tales to Terrify, Shock Totem, Amazing Stories,* and in the anthologies *Nemonymous* and *Chilling Ghost Stories* from Flame Tree Publications. He is a graduate of the Odyssey Writers Workshop.

Jae Steinbacher is a queer nonbinary trans writer and editor. They have been published in *The Magazine of Fantasy & Science Fiction*, *PodCastle*, *Terraform*, and elsewhere. Jae is a graduate of the Clarion West Writers Workshop and North Carolina State University's MFA program. You can find them on Twitter @JaeSteinbacher.

Susan Taitel would like you to believe that she knows how to write a pithy author bio. If that does not sound plausible maybe you could be convinced that she is from Chicago and would like to write a pithy author bio but will settle for a dryly amusing author bio. However if that is too much of a stretch, you could consider that she lives in Minnesota and never breaks into a cold sweat at the words "author bio." If you are foolish enough to believe that, you can find more of her lies in *Cast of Wonders, Galaxy's Edge Magazine,* and *Cossmass Infinities* as well as on her website susantaitel.com.

Izzy Wasserstein is a queer, trans woman who teaches writing and literature at a midwestern university and writes poetry and fiction. Her work has appeared in *Clarkesworld Magazine, Apex Magazine, Fireside Magazine,* and elsewhere. She shares a home with her spouse, Nora E. Derrington, and their animal companions. She's an enthusiastic member of the 2017 class of Clarion West.

Rem Wigmore is a speculative fiction writer based in Aotearoa New Zealand, author of the queer solarpunk novel *Foxhunt,* published by Queen of Swords Press, and forthcoming sequel *Wolfpack.* Their other works include *Riverwitch* and *The Wind City,* both shortlisted for Sir Julius Vogel Awards. Rem's short fiction appears in several places including *Capricious Magazine, Baffling Magazine* and the *Year's Best Aotearoa New Zealand Science Fiction & Fantasy* anthology. Rem's probably a changeling, but you're stuck with them now. The coffee here is just too good. Rem can be found at remwigmore.com or on twitter as @faewriter.

A. B. Young has spent the year haunted by the possums living in their roof. As they fall asleep at night, sometimes they think the scratching is coming from inside their head. They have named the possums Gilbert and Gubar. Young has been published in *Lady Churchill's Rosebud Wristlet*, *Heroines Anthology*, and was one of the 2019 winners of the PEN/Robert J. Dau Short Story Prize for Emerging Writers. They tweet at @theunrealyoung.

About Baffling Magazine

Baffling Magazine is a quarterly online magazine of flash fiction that publishes fantasy, science fiction & horror stories with a queer bent. Stories are first shared online with our patrons throughout the year. If you'd like to support us, please visit patreon.com/neonhemlock.

Visit us online at bafflingmag.com and on Twitter at @bafflingmag.

About the Press

Neon Hemlock is a Washington, DC-based small press publishing speculative fiction, rad zines and queer chapbooks. We punctuate our titles with oracle decks, occult ephemera and literary candles. Publishers Weekly once called us "the apex of queer speculative fiction publishing" and we're still beaming.

Learn more about us at neonhemlock.com and on Twitter at @neonhemlock.